PROMETHEUS'
PRIESTESS

GWYNETH LESLEY

OUTSPOKEN INK PRESS

OUTSPOKEN INK PRESS

First published in New Zealand in 2021 by Outspoken Ink Press

Text copyright © Gwyneth Lesley, 2021
Cover image copyright © Jem Butcher, 2021
Interior illustrations & formatting © Gram Telen, 2021
Editor: Jessica Brown
Author image: © Johanna Elizabeth, 2020

A catalogue record for this book is available from the New Zealand Library.

ISBN: 978 0 473 58687 4

Printed and bound by IngramSpark

THE FEMME FATALE SERIES
BOOK #1:
PROMETHEUS' PRIESTESS

One for sorrow
Two for joy
Three for a girl
Four for a boy
Five for silver
Six for gold
Seven for a secret never to be told.

Seven.
Seven women are about to tell you their stories.
These are the stories that several women
in your world know all too well.

We are the women they told you were
misfortune, our myths distorted over time.
We are the women they kept silent for our secrets.

Where we were once considered fearlessness personified,
messengers, and guardians ... now
you consider us unlucky.

Tainted.
Thieving.

Yet you forget. You stole our stories first.
For it is we who comforted Jesus on the cross.
We who survived outside of Noah's ark.
We who drank the wine of gods.

Perhaps that is why you thought us
made of the Devil's blood.

But don't you know by now?
The Devil is the dark shepherd.
Shepherding you through your own pain.
A rite of passage – in the hope you reunite with God.

You haven't been listening.

So we'll have to tell you the stories again.

THE GREEK GODS
AND GODDESSES
(AND THEIR ASSISTANTS)
YOU WILL COME ACROSS

MOIRAI (THE FATES)
These three sisters are responsible for the threads of human life.

Clotho – Spins the thread and decides when a person is born and when a god or mortal is to be saved or put to death.

Lachesis – The measurer of the thread, who decides how much time is allowed for each being and is sometimes associated with destiny.

Atropos – Also known as Aisa, chooses the manner of death by cutting the threads. She is also the eldest of the Fates and often called 'the inflexible one'.

ZEUS

God of Gods, King, Father...
This god has a thing for thunder and lightning and has produced a fair number of children.

Hera
Goddess of women, marriage, family and childbirth.
Also known as the Queen of Heaven, Zeus' jealous wife (and technically his sister).

Prometheus
Titan God of fire.
A good friend of Zeus, he created humanity from clay for his friend. He is known amongst the other gods as a champion of humankind and for his gift – foresight. At the time of our story he has been serving a 2,000-year solitude sentence for offering the humans fire, though this will not be his greatest crime.

Athena
Goddess of wisdom and war.
Known for her strategy and discipline, Athena is the Goddess that was born out of her father Zeus' head after he swallowed her mother, while she was pregnant, whole. You could say that, quite literally, makes her the definition of 'her father's daughter'.

Aphrodite
Goddess of love, beauty, passion, and procreation.
Technically born of Uranus' (Zeus' grandfather) genitals and seafoam, Aphrodite should be considered Zeus' aunt. However, to keep Zeus in his seat of power, and with her father dead, she was adopted as his 'daughter'. It's left her with a slight complex to prove herself right over others.

ARTEMIS

Goddess of the hunt, the wilderness, wild animals, the moon, and chastity.

Her twin brother is Apollo, who we don't meet here, and she is also the half sister of Athena, Aphrodite, Ares, Hephaestus, Hermes, and Dionysus. Due to events prior to this story, Artemis was responsible for the death of Adonis (Aphrodite's favourite mortal lover or adopted son ... entirely possibly both) and so the two of them aren't on best terms in this book.

ARES

God of war, violence, male virility, and defender of the weak.
Lover (and technically great nephew or adopted stepbrother) of Aphrodite. Half brother of Athena, Artemis, Hephaestus, Dionysus, and Hermes.

PHOBOS

The son of Aphrodite and Ares, Phobos is the personification of fear and panic.

HEPHAESTUS

God of fire and of craftsmen.
Son of Zeus and Hera, husband of Aphrodite. A hunchbacked, ungrateful metalworker who no one in the family particularly likes.

Hermes

The herald and messenger of the gods.

A wonderful mediator, guide, and protector. Also a half brother to Athena, Aphrodite (and lover), Artemis, Ares, Hephaestus ... you get the picture.

Tyche

Goddess of fortune and chance.

Daughter of Aphrodite and Hermes, friend of Prometheus. This Goddess has repeatedly denied Dionysus' flirtations in the past and why this is important will become clear in this tale.

Dionysus

God of the grape-harvest, fertility and divine madness.

Half brother along with all the rest of Zeus' children, with a bitter crush on Tyche.

Others you may need to know ...

Lysia (Lysimache I)

The high priestess of Goddess Athena Polias

Chief of the lesser officials, she is responsible for supervising the protective city deity of Ancient Athens.

Circe

Witch, enchantress, alchemist, and minor goddess.

Renowned for her vast knowledge of potions and herbs and transformational skills in the Greek world.

Gaia

The personification of the Earth and one of the Greek primordial deities, aka Mother Earth.
Also, technically, Zeus' grandmother.

Hestia

Goddess of hearth and home.

Demeter

Goddess of the harvest, mother of Persephone.

Persephone

Goddess of agriculture, daughter of Demeter, wife of Hades.
She spends her time split between the Underworld (autumn and winter) and the Earth (spring and summer).

Hades

God of the Underworld and brother of Zeus.

Styx

The river of the underworld. The gods swear by her water as their most binding oath.

Pygmalion

A sculptor who had sworn off love, who then fell in love with his statue.

EROS
God of lust and primal sexual desire. Son of Aphrodite and Ares.

ADEPHAGIA
Goddess of gluttony.

HYBRIS
Spirit of insolence, violence, and outrageous behaviour.

NEMESIS
The goddess who enacts retribution against those who succumb to hubris, arrogance before the gods.

PLUTUS
God of wealth.

AERGIA
The personification of sloth, idleness, indolence, and laziness.

PHTHONOS
The personification of jealousy and envy.

LYSSA
The spirit of mad rage, frenzy, and rabies in animals.

DIKE
Goddess of justice and spirit of fair judgement.

IRIS
The personification of the rainbow and another messenger of the gods.

CHRONOS
Son of Uranus (Sky Father) and Gaia, King of the Titans, and the God of time.

PROMETHEUS'
PRIESTESS

I weep, my creations.
That you may know
The toil I took, the time, the care.
And yet my care, you "cured".

Each masterpiece adorned with adoration,
Yet here you are, cracking, wilting, dying
A Blaming Creation.

I can't help the poeticness of my profess,
Because how poetic your actions
How poetic your duress.

You've broken my heart.
An artist disturbed by his living art.

Prometheus

To Mary-Kate,
For unlocking muse magic I had long thought gone.

PROLOGUE

The tapestry of humanity lay threadbare, metres and metres of it stretched out, until it lay unfinished, on the wooden hallway floor. One of the threads had caught on a nail, not quite embedded in the floor, and torn slightly, creating a little pocket in the tapestry. It would become a vacuum where nothing would exist for that part of humanity. Apparently, the humans called it a 'black hole'.

Earlier in the work, much earlier, the tapestry had been full of life and colour. Emerald greens of the earth and lapis lazuli blues of the oceans were interwoven with autumnal reds, cherry-blossom pinks, and every colour in between. Recently though, the strings the Fates had been called to spin on the loom had been beige, dull greys, and obsidian blacks.

Humanity was dying.

The ends of the tapestry lay on the floor limply while the three sisters the Greek world knew as the Moirai, the Fates, stared at the ends of the threads, wishing them to spring to life of their own accord and knit together a new picture. Alas, the threads weren't magical. It was the work of the three sisters that made the tapestry what it was, and while they could sometimes be swayed to tell a story a particular way, sometimes the threads spoke of their own free will.

Clotho hunched over, her black cloak and hood giving her the impression of Death rather than the life she was responsible for selecting. For it was her who chose the threads, her who decided who lived. She did, however, get the choice to *not* pick up the threads again, effectively ending life as easily as she gave it. It was a point of contention amongst the sisters.

She sighed. It wasn't that she *wanted* humanity to die; it was simply the fact that something else was being called to be birthed forward. Fear.

"I have no desire to pick up another one of these wretched threads." She stared at the beige silks and obsidian blacks beside her in disgust. She may as well have been sitting next to a pile of hay and chewing on cud, so bland and distasteful was her job at the moment.

"Well, you must." Lachesis, her elder sister snapped as she measured out the latest thread with her rod and began to weave it into the tapestry. Unlike Clotho, she was dressed in a sheath of white as pure as the destiny she represented.

"The story is not finished and I cannot tease the tapestry out anymore until you pick up the next thread," she continued in that pragmatic way of hers that spoke of her position as the middle child. Not that the sisters had been children for eons. Now they were old women, if you could even call them that, hunched over a loom that creaked with unfathomable age.

Unspoken remained the words that the tapestry would remain forever dormant, lying on the floor like an abandoned sweater.

"Atropos, what say you?" Lachesis asked.

The eldest, and smallest, of the three sisters scowled, deep grooves marring a long-ago smooth forehead.

"It doesn't end nicely. How am I supposed to end something so ... unfinished?! No, you must continue Clotho."

The youngest of the three, and perhaps that was why she was in charge of the youthfulness of birth, huffed. Really, she thought, Atropos had no right to tell her what to do after all these years. Just because she had always chosen the manner of death and cut the threads didn't mean she got to be in charge of *everything*. But the eldest among them was stubborn to a fault and bossy with it. There was no changing her mind, Clotho grumbled, even as she admitted that her sisters were right.

While the beigeness of life had begun to bleed into most of the tapestry, the grey steel of the industrial and technological age of humanity apparent, the black obsidian had not yet taken over. Oh, at first it had just been wisps of black. That jagged edge of fear that was necessary for human survival. It gave the tapestry definitive structure as the scenes from history played out in real time.

Now ... now it looked like a thick oil stain had been smeared across the Fates' work until it trickled through life, through the remaining threads and onto the wooden floorboards. But the tapestry wasn't yet completely pitch black. Fear hadn't yet cloyed and choked the living breath out of humanity completely.

The occasional thread of gold had still managed to sneak its way into the tapestry. There was hope yet.

"What do you suggest we do then, Aisa?" Clotho asked.

The eldest sister shot her a sharp look. "I told you not to call me that anymore."

"Why ever not?" Clotho mused with a sly smile, knowing how her sister preferred her middle name that more accurately reflected her role of death in the family. "It's your given name."

Atropos pointed the pair of sharpened blades in her hand as if taking aim at her eye.

"Stop bickering like old women." Lachesis interrupted them. "She's clearly baiting you, sister. In all our eons you would think you would not fall for it every time."

It was true. They often squabbled amongst themselves, even now, about how the tapestry should play out, but today the frustration between the sisters was palpable. While sometimes they could be fickle, today the Fates were decidedly not playing games.

"Well?" Clotho asked.

"They are not ready to die," Atropos eventually replied. "We must call in another."

"This fear, it is a human affliction," Clotho pointed out. "Should we call in Prometheus? He did create them after all."

"If you ask me, it looks more like war," Lachesis said. "Maybe we should call in Athena instead."

"It is both," Atropos agreed, though her forehead remained in a deep frown. "But you know how awry the tapestry gets when Prometheus' foresight gets involved."

"I'd rather not have to keep unpicking and redoing the threads unless getting him involved becomes absolutely necessary," Lachesis agreed.

"Then it's settled. The threat of war is greater anyway. Let's call in Athena." Atropos decided.

Clotho nodded and picked up an olive-green thread.

CHAPTER I

Athena stared at the table in front of her, the words of the Moirai fresh in her mind. Before her was a browned-with-age spread, a map of the world ingrained into the fabric of the table. It was a large, ugly thing, taking up the majority of the room. The wooden top was scored with marks from the years Athena had planned, acted, and executed battle plans, while its dark wooden legs curled and gnarled their way to a sandy stone floor. The rest of the room was carved from stone too. Opposite the great doors, made of the same dark wood as the table, were huge archways that showed spectacular views of Athens from high in the mountains. There were no shutters, nothing to stop the elements from breaking in, but then Athena always said working with the elements was an essential part of strategy. Despite the exposure, the room was pristine. There were a few potted plants dotted around the room, and opposite the large war table on the east-facing wall, there, instead of a fireplace, stood a small freshwater fountain by the chaises where she would retire for the day, for she had always thought of water as far more intelligent an element than the bruteness of fire.

One of her tawny owls watched her with a cocked head, quizzically, for there were currently no war pieces, which were usually placed in a chess-like pattern, across the table that Athena was staring hard at.

"This is no ordinary battle," she told her companion. "The humans aren't fighting some known enemy. They're actually fighting themselves, their instincts."

The owl hooted.

"I have absolutely no idea how to win this battle," she muttered to the only confidant she would ever say such a thing out loud to, for to admit weakness was to invite the vultures of her family to vie for her place.

"There is one who might be able to shed some light on the matter. Fetch Aphrodite for me."

The owl hooted again, spread its wings the width of the windowsill, and took off with a powerful beat of its wings. Athena watched it until it was a speck against a light grey sky that reflected the colour of her own eyes.

An hour passed before Aphrodite appeared before her in a light white sheath that matched her hair – so translucent and dewy, it appeared as if she had walked out of the ocean … again. Athena rolled her eyes.

Aphrodite raised an eyebrow. "You called for me while I was bathing. What did you expect?" She draped herself over one of the chaises as she squeezed droplets of water onto the floor.

"Do you mind?" Athena glanced at the water on the floor.

"Not at all." Aphrodite dismissed with a wave of her hand and a sharp smile. Anyone who believed the Goddess of Love was anything less than a savage was a fool.

"Why have you called for me? The owl didn't say."

"Tell me of your son, Phobos of Fear. Does he still follow his father, Ares, around like a schoolboy?"

A warmth invaded Aphrodite's eyes. For all her petty, vengeful behaviour with lovers, there was one thing Athena could not deny her and that was that she loved her children.

"He and his twin brother are terrors – quite literally – but yes they still follow their father. Why do you ask?"

Athena relayed the conversation she had had with the Fates, the tapestry they had shown her, and the creeping fear spreading through the humans. Aphrodite hissed out a breath between pursed, rosy-red lips that were often laughing. Right now they were not. "I am afraid, dear sister, Phobos is not capable of such a feat."

"I thought as much."

The sisters shared a grim look. For while it was common knowledge that Athena was a goddess of war, many did not know how well-versed in the art of war Aphrodite was.

"You know the human scope of emotion better than anyone. After all, it was you who gifted them with emotional intelligence. Tell me, Aphrodite, how would you stop it?"

The Goddess of Love continued biting her full lower lip. "In truth, the only way I can see their own fear being eradicated is if they alchemise it."

"Into what?"

"All emotions transmute into their opposites. Sadness to joy, anger to acceptance, fear to love," Aphrodite explained impatiently.

"This is your remit then."

"Yes," Aphrodite said, rising to stand at the opposite end of the table to Athena. "But you know the ruling. Hera is still on a warpath and I, for one, would prefer to avoid her."

Athena scowled. "Surely you can put aside petty title squabbles for this?"

"It's not petty," Aphrodite countered petulantly. "Our stepmother might not like me being associated with the Queen of Heaven when she wants the title for herself, but that gave her no right to demand Zeus have me married off to that ... ogre."

Athena's scowl turned into a savage smile and a bark of a laugh. "Oh yes, how is that wretch of a husband of yours?"

"Just as wretched as you remember."

For while Hephaestus was currently married to Aphrodite, she had not been the first sister he'd had his eye on. Originally, he had been after Athena. But Athena – cunning, brilliant Athena – had vanished from their marital bed before it was consummated. Aphrodite, on the other hand, had experienced what she liked to call 'a momentary lapse of judgement'. After Hera had caved to her son's demands – and who fell for such a stupid trick as to be stuck to a throne? – Zeus had demanded Aphrodite be married off to Hephaestus as per his request. Her father had tried to reason that it would prevent other gods from fighting over her, but Aphrodite had *liked* other gods doing that. Still, she preened at the attention from Hephaestus at first. He may not have been the most attractive god, but he had lathered her with honour and attention, and when he had presented her with a beautifully adorned, saltire-shaped girdle that accentuated her breasts and enhanced her beauty, she had agreed to consummate the marriage.

It had been many moons – and lovers – since they had been that happy and Hephaestus' attitude now matched his ugly exterior. Aphrodite couldn't bear it, but she could bear a grudge.

"I blame you, you know," she said, laughing. "If Zeus had not borne you out of his head, Hera would have never felt the need to bear that great heffalump."

Athena shrugged. "She says she loves me. Until she says or does otherwise, I'll choose to use that to my advantage."

"What Hera feels for you is not love. She tolerates you as Zeus' favourite."

Athena let out a small smile at the acknowledgement she thought her sister couldn't see. They weren't sisters in truth, which is perhaps why Aphrodite could make the remark without seething in jealousy, unlike the rest of their siblings. She was technically Athena's great aunt, but politics in the family were rife and so she had been "adopted" by Zeus to keep the lineage all neat and tidy. No one could tell the difference anyway, for Aphrodite's skin was as pure a white as milk and with a glow that made her look ever-fertile. She would never look her years.

"Regardless of how I feel about Hera," Aphrodite continued, "and even if we did ignore the ruling that we can't meddle in the affairs of humans anymore, I can only gift them love. It won't transmute the fear. It will just mean they hold both at once. What you need is an alchemist."

Athena nodded in understanding. Hera had, more specifically, forbidden her husband from actively participating in the human realm, given his penchant for other beautiful women. She hated how Zeus had petted over them, cosseted them. The nymphs had been bad enough, but to keep follying with the humans? No, to that she'd put her foot down. But, so as not to embarrass him, Hera had made the decree for all Greek gods and goddesses alike. It had been in place for the last two thousand years, give or take a couple of extra centuries, for time meant little to immortals. Of course, that hadn't stopped Zeus or any of the rest of them meddling, but the decree had been declared as a rule in Olympus, nonetheless.

The unspoken rule remained. If you were going to meddle in the affairs of humans, it had to go unnoticed. It was why the humans didn't believe in them, the gods, anymore.

There was a quick three-tap knock on the door.

"Enter."

A wizened older woman shuffled into the room. Her hair, the colour of straw and curls cropped close to her head, was held together by a woven band that was detailed with snakes and olive branches intertwined and spoke of how she held the office of High Priestess for Athena.

"Ah Lysia, your arrival couldn't be any more opportune."

"My Lady, I come with matters of state you have been asked to oversee." She walked over to Athena's desk by the arched window closest to Athena and placed the papers exactly in the order of importance and in a precise spot so as not to disturb anything else on the desk. She then stepped back and bowed deeply to both goddesses.

"You would think," Athena muttered, "that after the Romans ransacked my office and we relocated here, I would have less to deal with."

"I've taken care of most of it, my lady. Your keen eye to make sure all is as it should be, as well as your seal, is all that is required."

"Ah Lysia, must you take your leave this season? You truly are one of the most adept high priestesses to hold my office." In truth, she was the tenth in her family to take the title of High Priestess. Athena would mourn her stepping away, but already Lysia's daughter was training to take her place so that she might have a reprieve. She had certainly earned it.

"I will leave you in capable hands, I promise. Is there anything else I can do for you, my lady?"

"Actually there is." Athena pinned her with an eerie stare, and despite their relationship and her slight shuffle, from old bones weary from work, Lysia stood column straight with rigid shoulders as a soldier might stand to attention. "Do we have any in the Athenai sisterhood who are skilled alchemists?"

The High Priestess closed her eyes momentarily, stepping into a mind palace of archives. So great was the depth and breadth of this woman's knowledge, Athena didn't so much as appear startled when she received a reply.

"I will have to confirm with the parchment records, but I believe you have one who travelled to study under Circe, the first witch."

"Who?"

"Amara."

"Amara ... I know that name. Why do I know that name?" Aphrodite interrupted.

"I believe she also served at one time under you, my lady." Lysia inclined her head in acknowledgement. This did startle the two sisters, and Athena's bright eyes swivelled to a woman whose intellect was as sound as her judgement.

"You are sure, Lysia?"

"Almost certain, my lady. What's more, she also had a brief stint in Artemis' court."

Aphrodite let out a sharp whistle between perfect pearly teeth. "How did she manage to serve under each of us without the others ever knowing?"

Priestesses were allowed to serve under whichever deity they chose, but to serve as a priestess was to find favour with the goddess you chose and to serve her for the period of time agreed. Most chose to serve only one for the span of her natural born life, when they were allowed to take mortals for priestesses, but there were the occasional immortal priestesses that could find such favour that, should she wish to be released, her lady would grant her those privileges.

"That I do not know. But she clearly has a steel spine if she could maintain her chastity after her stint in your court before cultivating courage in my war rooms," Athena said. For she would not have taken on a priestess whose maidenhood had been broken and Aphrodite was known to lavish her ladies with desires of the flesh as much as she was to dote on them with beauty and material gifts when they found favour.

"I remember her now," Aphrodite nodded gracefully. "Oh, she was a delight. A beautiful creature too, if I remember correctly."

"Someone who can hold polar opposites with such ease as to go unnoticed amongst the goddesses' courts must surely be a talented alchemist." Lysia looked at the two goddesses pointedly.

"You are right as ever, Lysia. Fetch her for me, would you?" Athena asked. The High Priestess bowed in acquiescence and excused herself from the room. When she left, silence stretched across the table between the two sisters. Eventually, Aphrodite spoke.

"You always strategise better when you think out loud," she admonished Athena. "I can practically feel your thoughts bursting against your head as I speak."

That head, which was usually adorned with a gold-plated Corinthian helmet, was free today, Athena's bronzed and honey-coloured hair falling in loose curls around her shoulders.

Athena blew out a sharp breath. "There is one major problem with sending an alchemist to Earth."

"Which is?"

"To send Amara to teach the humans alchemy, we would have to get her in a human body."

Aphrodite stared at her blankly and Athena sighed in frustration.

"How do you get an immortal in a mortal body? We can transfigure them into just about anything. We can turn *ourselves* into mortal form for a time, but I have never placed an immortal soul into a human body. Have you?"

Aphrodite pursed her lips while a cute furrow appeared between perfectly manicured eyebrows. She could not say she had. For it had never been done before. Prometheus had shaped their original bodies from clay, sealed them with Zeus' spittle and sintered them with the white fire of knowledge. Athena had breathed life into them and Aphrodite had gifted them with emotional intellect.

"You could strip her from her immortal skin and build a new mortal body around her."

Athena paused, tapping out a rhythm with her fingers on the table as she considered it.

"It's brutal but it could work. How would we get her to agree to it though?"

Aphrodite shrugged. Athena despaired at how mercurial she could be.

"Being gifted with a task of this magnitude by her lieges shows an incredible level of trust. What more could she want? It's the highest honour we can give."

"She might not want to be stripped of her immortality," Athena reasoned.

Aphrodite made a back-handed shooing motion in the air. "We can put her back if we claim her task is an apotheosis. After all, humankind will be benefited by her actions, no?"

"A rite of passage where she reclaims immortality she already has?"

"We could strip her of it simply for the fact she fooled each of us by omission by serving in three different temples."

"You know there is no spoken rule that says she cannot do that." The timbre of Athena's voice held a warning.

"An unspoken rule is still a rule."

"No, that is not fair or just."

Aphrodite rolled her eyes. "Fairness is not the judge of all fates."

"It is in this room. No, I will appeal to her sense of duty. Like you so eloquently stated, the act is an honour. Perhaps we could reward her with more than her immortality should she complete it."

There was another brief pause as Aphrodite considered her sister's proposal before nodding.

"Kleos, a gift of glory, to cement her place in Olympic history. Yes, I will think of a suitable reward."

"Good. In the meantime, we shall need help with the human vessel to put her in. Let us pray that Prometheus is in the mood for an audience."

Aphrodite laughed and, unlike her sister's bark, it was a trillion trills that reminded anyone in its vicinity of tiny bells ringing. "That man is never in the mood for an audience."

CHAPTER II

L ysia appeared in the doorway of the Athenai temple.
It was not what it once was. When the Romans had
ransacked their lands and left their buildings to do little
more than crumble and become tourist attractions, the
sisterhood had been forced to flee. Now they resided in a
collection of small huts on the edge of Athena's estate that
were beautifully kept. The main area for the sisters' gathering
was little more than a converted barn but the floors were
immaculately swept, the fires lit, the altars adorned with
bountiful flowers, fruits, and dried meats in service to their
goddess. Even the air around them seemed sweet yet sharp
like the citrus trees outside, an apt way to describe those
that served Athena.

"Amara?" The high priestess called, her calm authoritative
voice echoing off the walls.

A priestess, who had been showing a younger woman how
to crush berries with the side of a blade to make a particular
tonic, looked up. A spark of recognition in her sharp green

eyes had her wiping her blade on her tunic, placing it down, and making her way calmly, yet efficiently, to the doorway.

"Lysia, I did not know we were to be expecting you. Please come in. May I offer you some refreshment? We purified the water today."

Lysia let out a chuckle as she acquiesced and walked to the seating area by the main circular altar. "Still using those herbal tricks Circe taught you I see."

"My Lady holds no complaint, does she?" Amara asked, a small smile on her face. But her voice held a thread of worry. Ah, but Amara made a good priestess because she cared what her liege thought of her.

Lysia smiled. "She does not. In fact she has a task for you."

Before she could reveal anymore, two other women approached them.

"Amara, we were smoking the wood as you showed us but the flame licked too high and now these meats are ruined. What shall we do? Athena hates burnt meat and it is too charred for the sisters to eat," the younger of the two asked.

"Excuse me," Amara said to Lysia before cupping the younger, more hysterical, woman's face in her hands. "We shall fix it."

"How?" the other asked.

Amara took the meat from their hands. "Go and fetch me a bowl from the kitchens."

When they returned, Amara placed the meat in the bowl and poured over the water she meant to drink with Lysia.

"Cut some of the citrus fruits from outside and get some of the freshly crushed berries your sister is working on in the kitchens. Add it to this bowl. Place a lid on it and then sit it on the smoking wood *away* from the flames. It should soften and thicken into a nice broth for us tonight."

"Thank you, Amara," the older and taller of the two said.

"You're welcome," she nodded before sending them on their way and returning to her seat with Lysia.

"You would have made an excellent high priestess," Lysia observed with a keen eye.

"Politics and paperwork are not my forte," Amara countered with a warm smile.

"Yet leadership is, for the others come to you for guidance."

"I think they are so used to strategy sometimes that they forget simplicity."

"You are being modest," Lysia chided. "What you do is no simple parlour trick. It is alchemy."

"That was cooking," Amara replied dryly.

"Cooking is a basic form of alchemy," Lysia countered.

Amara was silent for a moment, contemplating her answer.

"Sometimes I wonder, if Hestia were to take her seat amongst the twelve gods, perhaps I would have only served her instead and then all they would say of me was that I ran a good household."

"Is that what you want? To run a good household?"

"Yes," said Amara, but that wistful tone in her voice gave her away once again.

"Yet here you are in Athena's lands. Why?"

"I wished to learn courage."

"For what purpose?"

"The quiet courage it takes to be a woman who loves simply at home is just as important as the courage on the battlefield," Amara replied quietly, for that was not a popular opinion amongst the Athenai who went about their daily rituals around them. Most longed to be more like their goddess, to counter their sweet temperament that had not always served them well. There was nowhere else for a woman to learn courage such as Athena taught.

"Ah. And so the stint with Aphrodite was to teach you the love you wished to cultivate?"

Amara nodded.

"And Artemis before that?"

"She taught me how to be at one with nature."

Lysia smiled, understanding dawning in her mind at the young priestess' moira, *her destiny*. She would run much more than just a household, a sisterhood, the Fates whispered. These skills were destined for something greater.

Amara looked at Lysia, trepidation pacing behind her eyes at the woman's silence.

"You won't tell Her, will you?"

To be in service to multiple goddesses for your own gain was taboo and Amara had nowhere else to go, no family. She'd been the unfortunate offspring of her mother's rape, abandoned in the fields of Artemis as a babe. Priestesshood, servitude, was all she had ever known.

"I have no need to. Athena summons you for a task. It would appear your skills are about to serve you as they were always intended to."

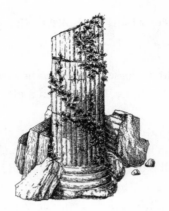

CHAPTER III

Prometheus rumbled a deep, exasperated sigh as he watched the bobbing head of a visitor come up the steep track that followed the olive groves and dips in the valley below him before reaching his cabin. His home was high enough up in the Parnitha mountains that he didn't usually get guests, which was the point, but he already had an inclination about who was approaching him and knew that this would be no social visit.

Bracing himself on the dark red oak desk he'd carved, sanded, and polished this past summer, he rose and walked barefoot across wooden floorboards made of the same oak as he continued to watch his guest effortlessly make her way up the mountainside that was still basking in the late afternoon Grecian sun. It was just beginning to dip below the hills in the distance, creating a shadowed effect across the land that had turned it golden after the hottest summer Prometheus could remember. Demeter, Goddess of the Seasons, had enjoyed a delightful six months reunited with her daughter, Persephone, who now returned to the underworld with Hades. It had been a glorious, if brutal, summer.

Squinting against the light, convinced his eyes were playing tricks on him, he noticed that he had not one guest but two. The taller of the two he recognised immediately. It was hard to mistake Athena's six-foot two-inch slender frame and confident gait. The petite, curvier woman, who walked behind her, he did not recognise. Both finally made it up to the top of the dusty track to await him in the courtyard.

"You've begun new projects," Athena stated in lieu of an introduction, nodding towards the blossoming vegetable patch to her left and the metalwork on her right that Prometheus still hadn't put back in his workshop yet.

"Idle hands," he replied in turn, holding up a pair of hands the size of baseball mitts in surrender. They were tanned and calloused from his projects, with a light dusting of dark brown hair on the back of them that grew deeper and darker as they made their way up strong forearms. Those hands gestured that Athena and her companion would be welcome to enter his home, though he didn't really want them in his space, accompanied by a ground-out, between-clenched-teeth "please".

Athena nodded and moved swiftly inside, the younger woman following behind with her head bowed. Her eyes – bright, inquisitive cat-green eyes – glanced at Prometheus briefly as she passed through the doorway, before quickly darting back down to the ground. He watched Athena taking stock of everything in the rooms, swivelling her head with each stride until she finally found herself in the kitchen, which had a door leading out the back to a patio and a stunning brickwork island.

"Idle hands indeed," she murmured, for it had not looked like this the last time Athena had visited.

Square jaw dusted with dark stubble clenched, Prometheus chose to ignore the barb. Athena probably hadn't meant it the way it sounded, seeing as she was patron of household craft. Instead, he set about putting together a platter of meats, olives, and cheeses with wine, as it was custom to provide guests with the goods of hospitality no matter if you were the Titan that had birthed the goddess from Zeus' head and had no idea of who the other strange creature was with her.

The two women sat in companionable silence as Prometheus plated up and set the feast in front of them, for he was not a man of small talk.

"Who are you?" he gruffly asked, as he placed a ceramic plate in front of the young woman who still hadn't shared her identity yet.

"Oh, I am Amara." She smiled. It was a smile so pure, one that lit up the corners of her eyes until they shined, that Prometheus found his own eyes crinkling in turn as he smiled back.

"A pleasure, Amara. Please, eat."

Prometheus remained standing on the other side of the brickwork island while Amara obliged her host and Athena helped herself too, as she neatly bit prosciutto-wrapped asparagus tips and methodically worked her way through two, following it with a sip of wine. Having fulfilled the custom of being a gracious guest, just as Prometheus had followed the custom of being a hospitable host, she played what Prometheus imagined was her opening gambit, to gauge how well he had fared in the years since he'd been banished from Olympian society.

"Were you aware that the Panathenaic festival passed through here not even two decades ago? They still run your torch relay, you know. Though humans call it the Olympic Games now."

Prometheus had begun shaking his head before she'd even finished. "You know I have no interest in games that are all about politics," he replied quietly, the deep timbre of his voice holding a sense of certainty that couldn't be shaken.

Athena closed her eyes and took a deep breath. "I did not come here to quarrel, Prometheus."

He regarded the goddess for a moment. They had been close once, when being part of the mortal world was allowed. Together they had aided some of the greatest philosophers and built civilizations that were still marvelled at today. They hadn't always agreed, mind you. Prometheus knew Athena's tactics for strategy, knew too her penchant for riling him up when he could usually keep a cool head. For if he was the fire, she was the air that whipped him into biting back and the water that doused his flame when he got going.

"Why did you come here, Athena?"

And why had she bought a guest?

"Has word reached you of what is going on in the human realm?"

Prometheus shook his head again. "Zeus' eagle still circles. I am essentially under house arrest."

Amara hissed in a breath at hearing the ancient confirm what had only been rumoured, that his punishment from Zeus for giving the humans the element of fire had not been the rock but a shunning from society, and proceeded to choke on an olive. While Athena shot her a glare, Prometheus smiled wryly and pushed her cup of wine closer towards her. Amara clutched at it and washed down the vestiges of the olive that had caused such a display.

"Sorry," she gasped.

"It is quite alright, child." Prometheus chuckled.

At Athena's inquisitive gaze, he realised he had not chuckled since the last time he was in the presence of humans. It was an ... odd sound to hear again from his own throat.

"What has been going on in the human realm?" He turned to ask Athena.

"Fear eats at them," Athena informed him. "It's a dry rot that lurks beneath their skin. They age slower but die faster. They live longer but their lives are blander. They create but never replenish. In their desperation to guarantee their survival, they actually push themselves closer to extinction. Each collective move takes them one step further into the abyss.

"They're killing Gaia too. You know her patience usually knows no bounds but even she has a tipping point. She has become restless, heaving underneath human feet while conversing with Uranus, Zeus' grandfather and our Sky

Father. You must have felt it."

Prometheus' eyes turned dark.

"I warned Zeus this would happen," he said quietly.

"You did?"

"When Hera banished us from the human realm," he continued, "I knew the humans would rely on the tools we taught them – science, medicine, legality ... you know how they watched us, like a child watches a parent to learn what we do. But when we left, they had no one but themselves to turn to."

"And so the fear that was supposed to keep them alive, keep them safe from us, was turned in on themselves," Athena finished.

"Exactly." Prometheus nodded, moving his big hands through curls that brushed the nape of his neck.

"They won't survive three centuries," Athena told him and for this she received a look of deep, unfathomable pain.

"You're certain?"

"Yes," she said softly, knowledge in her eyes that said she knew the trick Aphrodite had played on him all those years ago. "I have a plan."

Prometheus' jaw tightened again. "No, Athena. I know you. You will treat this like it is war."

"It is."

"No, it is a human affliction. The Moirai should never have dragged you into this."

"Well they have and I will not have one of my father's precious creations – albeit by your hand – be destroyed. As an old friend, I came to ask for your help."

"In what?"

Athena paused and looked at Amara, who had been quietly eating and sipping her wine, watching two ancients discuss human civilization like it was a chess match. It was fascinating. No priestess was ever given such a rare honour. When Lysia had taken her to Athena and the goddess had outlined the task she had wanted Amara to undertake, every cell in her body had screamed yes, that this was her destiny, that she'd finally be who the Fates wanted her to be. But when both sets of eyes bored into her, she suddenly realised that being close to two gods, one a Titan no less, was perhaps not an honour so much as potentially a very poor survival move on her behalf.

"Amara here is the most talented alchemist left in Olympus."

Prometheus grunted. "Is that so?"

He stared at Amara under bushy brows as if considering something before reaching for her glass. He turned and filled the remaining half with water. Half water, half wine, he returned the glass in front of Amara. Instinctively, she knew what he was asking of her.

Closing her eyes, she placed both hands on the stem of the glass. Repeating the incantation in her head until every fibre of her being believed that she would taste pure wine when she lifted the cup to her mouth, Amara felt the cells change in her fingertips and travel up the thick glass stem made of pure crystal. Only when she was certain that the process was completed – that the glass now only contained wine once again – did she open her eyes and push it across the island to Prometheus.

Not taking his eyes from her, he picked up the glass and drank. When it was finished, he placed it back down and wiped at lips that Amara couldn't seem to tear her eyes from. They were full-bodied and when he spoke, the voice that came out of them made every cell of her being fidget in attention. She watched him, half fascinated and half terrified. His face revealed nothing until he said, "You are talented indeed."

"Amara has agreed to be placed on Earth to teach the humans the art of alchemy. To transmute the fear into love. She will lead the next lineage of witches, and this time we will have her go in human form so as not to arouse suspicion. We don't need another century of witch-hunting," Athena told him.

"Ah and so you ask me for a human cloak for her?"

"If it is indeed possible."

Prometheus didn't answer, but instead turned to Amara.

"What happens if you fail in your task?"

"The fear will eat me alive in my human form," she replied softly.

Prometheus' brow furrowed, lines straining his dishevelled, tanned face. Rugged in a way that appealed to warrior goddesses and also those who preferred not to get their hands dirty, Prometheus had the mark of a man who spent his time farming the land. Built with muscle that only came from manual labour, no one would look at Prometheus and think of an artist if they did not know him. Especially not one who was so meticulous about each of his human creations that he sculpted from large, calloused hands with the utmost care.

"And if she is caught by one of the gods?" This question he addressed to Athena.

"She is not a god. Therefore she does not break the meddling rule."

"Yet you send her into the human world to do your bidding," Prometheus countered, a quiet rage beginning to simmer beneath his words. Athena had a terrible habit of treating humans as little more than chess pieces. The fact that she would do so with such a delicate creature as that which sat across from him, irked him. There was something about Amara that he couldn't quite put his finger on. Something about her that made his instincts pay attention.

"The rule is clear. The Gods of Olympus cannot meddle in the affairs of humans. There was nothing to be said of anyone or anything else. Surely you of all people appreciate the loophole?"

He cast Athena a dirty look that said he knew what she was playing at and, instead, he turned his attention back to Amara.

"And what have you been offered for such an undertaking?"

Amara glanced at Athena for permission to share and received a nod.

"The great goddesses have offered me a place among history that few have received. Should I complete my moira, I shall receive a temple of my own. To share my gifts and arts with others. To become someone of note."

It was all anyone wanted in Olympus, to become someone that history remembered. Unspoken were the words that she would feel as if she had finally found purpose in this world.

Prometheus' eyes bored into her, as if trying to determine the truth behind her words, the motivation behind her actions. *As if he knew she was lying to herself.*

Apparently satisfied for now, he spoke once again. "Human souls are different from immortal souls. They only know the confines of the bodies I've built them. They have no sense of freedom the way we do. When their souls are freed, they are released back into the breath of air that swirls around us. That is a human's first true taste of freedom, not the free will they play with down there on Earth. Death circles their minds at all times. You have never known death. Once you are in a human body, we have no way of knowing if you'll retain your memories of Olympus enough to perform the alchemy. You may never again know the freedom you have now. What is being asked of you is dangerous."

"Someone has to teach the humans and I have faith. It got me this far." Amara replied softly, though her spine was as straight as steel as she gestured to the cup in front of him as proof of her abilities.

Something in Prometheus tugged low and deep in his belly. Instinct roared at him to protect her, to say no to the goddess' plan. But some primal part in the back of his mind said to watch, to wait, and, for some inexplicable reason, to trust Amara. He hadn't had cause to trust another in eons. It felt ... uncomfortable. But even her mere presence caused his concerns to ease somewhat. It was as if she was practising her alchemy on him. Though surely a priestess wouldn't dare influence a god without permission.

Finally he said to Athena, "You ask too much of her."

"And you make ominous declarations, as usual."

Athena continued when Prometheus went to rebut, "The ruling only speaks of the Gods of Olympus not getting involved with human life. You are a Titan. Hera has no say on what you can do. No one would even stop you walking through the mortal world given your role in their creation."

Prometheus cocked an eyebrow at Athena.

"You forget about Zeus' eagle."

"I will find a way to deal with my father if you agree to help," Athena promised, grabbing Amara's wrist and, turning the priestess' palm upwards, thrusting it towards Prometheus.

Moments passed in silence as Prometheus considered it, staring, unblinking, at Athena. But they both knew he was stalling. Athena had played her ace card when she had stated with certainty that the humans were dying. Prometheus' fate was already tied to theirs. It had been a long time ago.

Eventually he held out his own palm in turn next to Amara's, resigned to play the Moirai's games, even as a part of his brain clawed desperately at him not to.

"I will assist your priestess, Amara, on Earth to the best of my abilities. This oath I swear by Styx herself."

Taking a knife from the butter-soft sheath on her bicep, Athena sliced Amara's left palm from index finger to wrist before doing the same to Prometheus. To the priestess' credit, she didn't let out so much of a hiss as tears blinked into her eyes. They grabbed one another's forearm and his sworn oath was bound. The pact was sealed in ichor, the golden substance binding the two of them together in place of blood. Athena wiped the blade across old, worn warrior leathers and returned it to its sheath. It was done.

CHAPTER IV

Twenty-five years later ...

Amara had been left as a baby, wrapped in a thick tartan scarf, on the church doorstep she now stood under to escape from the rain. The limestone of the doorway arch she leant against was smooth and worn with age. Many feet had crossed this threshold, more than just the ones Amara had known in her twenty-five years of existence. The red wooden door she had knocked on had been in desperate need of a coat of paint since she could remember. In front of her, the stone-paved road sat at an intersection.

To her left, the street would take you along shop windows that sparkled with designer names above the door, and window displays that dripped with money and excess. On her right, across the road, was the cute bistro where she had just finished her shift for the day. In summer she served quaint wooden tables with red and white chequered tablecloths dotted around outside, but the drizzle and bite of winter wind had driven almost everyone inside today.

Amara watched the few remaining people on the street escape to shelter. The first, a Parisian woman whose accent coloured the air as she spoke violently fast French into a mobile phone, teetered in six-inch heels as she made her way into the bistro. As the woman walked through the doors to the bistro, an old couple passed her on their way out. The man, who was balding and whose jacket barely stretched over his belly to reach his waist, opened up an umbrella under the awning for his grey-haired love as they made their way across the street to a taxi. She wondered about the lives of the strangers she watched, their families, what their homes were like, as she always did when she was people watching.

Twenty-five years she had lived in Paris and though she loved it, it had never felt like home. Instead, her life felt like the crossroads in front of her. Colourful characters surrounded her, but her life felt empty. Everyone else seemed to have their own lives and here she was simply seeking shelter from the rain and cold. *There had to be more to life,* she reasoned with herself. It was a constant feeling that nagged at her. If she chose one path, she could end up with riches as if she walked down the left street or she could turn right and forever live a life of servitude, like her job at the bistro. She worried if she pulled at the wrong thread of life that it would all unravel and she'd end up back here. Not in a physical sense. She loved Paris. It was a bright jewel, truly the City of Lights. But her mind was a dark place, a decidedly unpleasant place to be. It kept warning her that time was running out and in the back of her mind, there was a voice constantly nagging at her to *do something*. She just couldn't figure out what that *something* was.

The door behind her opened.

"Come in, my child. Get out of the cold." Father Michel spoke in fluid French as he ushered her in.

"Thank you, Father," she replied in the same tongue.

Once inside she could see he was setting up for evening Mass and so she quickly got to work with the grape juice and crackers, though she still didn't take off her red wool coat, as the church was draughty with its lofty windows and terrible insulation. For her troubles, she received a small smile that lit up the eyes of the man she had always considered her father, even though she had grown up at the orphanage across the river.

He had been the only constant in her life and had not aged in all the time she'd known him, not truly. His hands were still the same broad, dark tanned hands that had always held her as she cried, though now they had a few more liver spots. His stubble on a round face that spoke of a man who ate well was speckled with grey now, but only if she looked closely. His nose and brow were wide but his eyes were deep, a never-ending brown that could see into depths of her she wasn't quite sure even she was ready to look at yet.

"Ah, my Amara. Always so dependable and reliable."

The unexpected words, a balm for her earlier train of thought, caused a lump in her throat to rise and tears stung at her eyes. How could she even be thinking of leaving this man who had practically raised her when she was not his own? She desperately tried to blink away the tears as quickly as they had appeared but it was too late. As always, Father Michel missed nothing.

"What upsets you, my child?"

Amara continued fiddling with the thumb-sized plastic cups, keeping her hands busy. But when Father Michel pressed a hand to her shoulder in a show of affection, the dam broke and the tears fell rapidly down golden skin that was dusted with freckles. Father Michel didn't say anything as tears continued to pour down her cheeks until she impatiently wiped them away. Then he steered her towards the direction of a pew and had her sit, taking her hands in his.

"Come, tell me what troubles you."

Eventually, between gulped tears, while Father Michel patiently waited and continued to stroke her arm, Amara answered.

"I-I-I don't think I'm supposed to be here anymore," she said in a whisper.

He was quiet for a moment. Then he said, "I had a feeling this day would come. I just did not expect it so soon."

"You did?" Amara whispered without looking at him. She hadn't realised that she had been seeking more than sanctuary and a familiar face when she knocked on the door after her shift. She had been seeking, as always, answers, in strong arms that could hold her when she felt like she was breaking.

"You are always so shocked that others know you. Yet you wear your heart so openly on your sleeve," he admonished as he stroked said sleeve and cradled her to him. Amara scowled against his chest even though he couldn't see, for she did not like to openly admit to anything so vulnerable.

Yet tears welled up in her eyes again when he said, "I would not begrudge you a life of adventure to stay and keep an old man like me company. You are reliable and dependable because you are Amara, not because of what you do or do not do. Can you not see that?"

She shook her head, and dark curls that were usually tied up in a bun escaped and buzzed around her forehead like bees. Father Michel sighed and leaned back in the pew.

"Did you know, when you were around five you escaped the clutches of your latest foster mother? May she rest in peace. She came looking for you here that day, convinced you'd come to see me. Together we found you at a bakery a kilometre from your home. When we found you, you told me you were chasing the smell of heaven."

"I don't remember that." Amara hiccupped.

"I don't suppose you do. You were very young. My point being, child, you are as reliable as you are wild and as dependable as you are independent. They are both two sides of the same coin. One cannot exist without the other."

Amara thought about that for a moment before Father Michel continued. "But above all, you have always been an explorer."

"The explorers you told me about in stories always come across monsters though. What if leaving is a terrible idea? Why aren't you talking me out of it?" she demanded, almost desperately.

Father Michel smiled.

"We humans are funny creatures. We still believe the Devil and his monsters cause bad things to happen to us."

"Don't they?" Another hiccup.

"Do you not listen to any of my sermons, child?" He admonished Amara with a smile. She pulled back and made a face at him before he dragged her back in for another hug. In truth she was an avid note-taker in the sermons. Her devotion to something *other* had never been in question, not since Father Michel had known her.

"The way I see it, the Devil and his demons have a bad reputation. After all, he was the fallen angel of God, the favourite. What if between the two of them they agreed that the Devil would be sent down to Earth to do the dirty work? What if the dirty work is a way to turn us closer to God? Besides, there can be no light without dark. What a thankless task he has. What grace it must take to do the dirty, unappreciated work that could actually help us." Father Michel paused. "If only we didn't use demons or monsters as crutches."

Amara bit her full lower lip. She knew what he was getting at, but still ...

"I'm scared."

"I know, child. That's a good thing. It will keep you safe."

"I thought you just said monsters weren't bad things?" She teased.

"That doesn't mean I want to see you hurt." He squeezed her tighter.

Eventually she said, "You're not mad at me for wanting to leave?"

"How can I be mad at a part of you I love?"

A brief silence fell between them, heavy with the weight of memories, until Father Michel spoke once again.

"Where will you go?"

"Scotland," Amara said immediately, with such confidence and clarity that she suddenly realised this was what she had been mulling over in agony all this time. Not where she would go but what she would leave behind.

"You still believe that the tartan you were wrapped in as a babe has something to do with your birth parents? A message of some kind?"

"I don't know." Amara shrugged, though that was a lie to herself more than anyone else. It was why she kept the tartan in question always neatly folded at the bottom edge of her bed. The tug in her gut when she saw it every morning was a visceral thing, the thread of life that pulled at her.

At that moment, the winds began to whistle through the church melodically. They felt like a siren call to Amara that she couldn't begin to put into words. All she knew was that she wanted to chase the wind's tail until she arrived at the destination she was, for want of better words, destined for.

"It would seem as if the winds are calling you," Father Michel said, a twinkle in his eye. Amara sat up and peeked at him from behind long eyelashes and eyed him warily. Occasionally, she was convinced he could actually read her mind. He chortled.

"Ah, you are an open book child."

She nudged him playfully with her shoulder and he wrapped an arm around her again until she leant in fully for a cuddle. His torso was squishy, but his arm around her was firm ... as if there was strength of steel beneath the soft layer of fat he held. The rough material of his jumper scratched at her cheeks but she didn't mind. Always, this man had been her solid, dependable rock.

"When will you go?"

"I'm not sure yet," she whispered. "Soon I think, but I'll come back." Though they both knew she wouldn't know when, and he could likely be dust on the wind, Father Michel smiled and agreed.

"I'll see you when you're back."

"And I'll write to you."

"I shall await stories of your adventures with eager anticipation." A muzzled kiss pressed to her forehead.

"I don't know exactly where I'll end up."

"Do any of us?"

Finally Amara said, "I'm still scared, Father."

"Ah." His grip tightened on her shoulder fiercely. "We're all a little scared, child, but the best adventures come with a little risk."

CHAPTER V

"I warned Athena this might happen." Prometheus said, staring at an incredulous Aphrodite.

"Why did you let it happen? That's what I want to know."

Prometheus grimaced, a vein pulsing in his neck, at having to answer the one woman he swore he'd never be in the same room as again. That room was once again Athena's war room; the only neutral place the three had agreed to meet in.

"There was no other way to integrate the priestess into society other than to place her in the body of an infant. We knew there would be a possibility, because the brain had to grow from scratch, that her soul would retain its essence but not its memories."

"We couldn't be sure at first," Athena continued on from him calmly, "but now that her human function is fully developed, it would appear our suspicions were right. Her Olympian memories are either gone or trapped in some deep recess."

Twenty-five years had been nothing to the gods to wait to see if Amara had matured into a woman capable of wielding the power of alchemy. It seemed a small portion of time to them, considering there would be at least another three centuries before humanity died out, given their current predicament. Gaia wasn't yet completely sick of them and extinction was a long and tedious process.

"If her memories are there, how do you unlock them?" Aphrodite asked.

"It's likely," Prometheus continued, "that her Olympian memories will be tied to her instincts. In order to access them, we are going to have to challenge her to follow them without question."

"How would you suggest we do that?"

"You were the one who suggested we place her in the City of Light, Aphrodite. We were hoping you had some idea of what would cause her to want to leave? If we can tap into that thread she's following, we can exploit it and help her unlock those memories instinctively."

"If they are there," Aphrodite said.

Prometheus nodded once. "Correct."

"The fact she wants to leave Paris, despite all her emotional ties being there, suggests our suspicions are correct – her instincts are driving her where we want her to go. We just need you to confirm them," Athena added.

There had been great debate between the three of them over where to place Amara originally. Prometheus had reasoned it was logical to place her in Greece. It would give her the strongest tie to her heritage and therefore to her alchemy skills. Athena, ever strategising, decided it was too great a threat to place her so directly in the eyesight of the gods. And then Aphrodite had countered them both with a suggestion they hadn't expected would work.

"Why not? It's close enough on the European continent to keep her tied to her power. It's the city of love, which is what she's there to transmute the fear into, and the whole process is designed to drive out the dark stain of fear in humanity, isn't it? Where better than the City of Light?"

Prometheus and Athena had looked at one another astounded. Meanwhile Aphrodite had brandished a coy and cunning smile.

"Love is more than capable of existing with logic. How many times do I have to tell the pair of you?"

Prometheus' brow had darkened, for he knew very well why love and logic could not coexist together, thanks to Aphrodite. It was not an intellectual battle he was prepared to have with her. Not again.

Back in the present, Aphrodite closed her eyes and tuned into the frequency of Amara's aura, as she could with any human in the world. "I can't quite say for certain what has caused her to want to leave the city. It's ... muddy. But then, humans' processes always are. The only thing I can say is it is not only an emotional pull that drives her. There's something it's entwined with. I can't see what. That's all I can tell you." Aphrodite shrugged, an elegant movement that made Prometheus think of water rippling down a river.

"It's highly likely," Athena said, looking at Prometheus, "that the tether you can't see is instinct. We should ask

Artemis for her help. She was the one that moulded Amara's instincts after all."

"Must we get her involved?" Aphrodite butted in, a scowl gracing her face.

"You know she is well acquainted with instinct even better than Prometheus or I. Not to mention her history with Amara," Athena admonished in a way that was both gentle and condescending in equal measure.

Athena had told Prometheus what she'd learned of Amara's past through Lysia's digging. While she had seemed initially angry, it now appeared the goddess of strategy was willing to use it to her advantage. And to do that, Prometheus knew she would rope in whoever she needed to.

Turning to her desk, she pulled out a fresh sheet of parchment. Dipping the quill into dark ink, she scrawled a note, rolled it, pressed her seal and then gestured for today's owl to fly forward. The snow-white owl hooted and flew towards one of the leather raptor clasps that adorned both of Athena's forearms.

"Take this to Artemis, no delays."

He blinked once in understanding before shuffling slightly on his talons, as if to find his footing, and then took off through the arched windows.

"Artemis should be with us within three days once she has the note."

"Why bother? We could offer Amara white fire. The manifestation of the knowledge of the Gods would bring her soul's knowledge to the surface of her skin," Aphrodite suggested petulantly, and in vain.

"That is a foolish suggestion even from you," Prometheus replied, at his wit's end with her need to always get her way.

Aphrodite's eyes narrowed in anger and she opened her mouth to spit a retort when he continued. "Do you remember when I presented them with the element of fire? Do you recall what happened then?"

It was a rhetorical question, of course. Both Athena and Aphrodite had been present for the creation of Pandora. Aphrodite herself had cast the woman in her image and her attendants had lavished her in gold silks and jewellery while Athena had breathed life into her. The poor, unsuspecting girl had been sent to Earth – to Prometheus' brother as a bride – with a box that should have never been opened. But Zeus, insecure and loath to trust, had decided if the humans could have all the elements his grandmother offered, then they could have all the evils of the world too.

He hadn't spoken to Prometheus since.

"If we give her the knowledge of the white fire and that's how she chooses to teach the humans to alchemise fear, we may as well wipe them all out now and save Zeus the trouble," Prometheus told her.

Aphrodite might profess to be the Goddess of Love but she was nothing more than a manipulative witch who cared for no one but herself, he thought darkly. He'd walk through the halls of Hades before he let her get her way. And she well knew why.

"We will wait for Artemis. Then we will decide," Athena declared.

Three days later, Artemis strode along the footpath towards Athena in a plain brown warrior tunic made of the finest-quality leather. It crossed over one shoulder and fit snugly to her small-busted torso before falling into pleated leather slits at the knees, allowing her freedom of movement. Across her back was slung a quiver laced with intricate gold detailing of cypress leaves and the sigils of the hunting dog, the stag, and deer – her hunting pack, Artemis called it. At her feet, two hounds bounded along to keep up with her long strides.

"Athena." The sisters greeted and clasped forearms in the old ways of the warrior. Artemis' hunting abilities had made her, on occasion, useful to Athena's plans and she was one of the best advisers the Goddess of Wisdom knew, provided she wasn't offering counsel on someone who had disrespected the family. Then she tended to be somewhat ... ferocious.

Athena had decided it was best for them to meet alone, for while Prometheus and Artemis had no quarrel the same could not be said of her two sisters. Last Athena had heard, Artemis still pined for her mortal beloved that Aphrodite had killed, and there was a nasty rumour Artemis was responsible for the death of Aphrodite's adopted son, Adonis, in turn. Not that she would ever admit to it, but then you wouldn't. Aphrodite had a cruel streak if you crossed her that would cause even a rabid wolf to whelp in pain. Far better to let rumours go unconfirmed and to keep those two as far away from one another as possible.

"Come, let us walk in the gardens." Athena knew how much Artemis hated sitting still when she could roam. And the gardens were fields of vast land, untouched for kilometres except by Athena's trusted Guard that maintained the property. The rolling hills were expansive, dipping with crevices in some areas, providing spectacular views of Athens in others. Artemis' hounds ran ahead as she shot arrows for them to chase.

"Those are fine quality," Athena remarked. "A gift from Hephaestus, like the quiver?"

"Indeed. Aphrodite's husband was most generous." Artemis smirked, and Athena got the impression he would have made the arrows for Artemis after news of Adonis' death and his wife's sorrow. Spite, it seemed, was a trait he shared with his wife.

Instead, Athena commented, "Those better not hit any of my horses."

"When have you ever known me to be so careless?" Artemis took the arrow from one of her hounds and shot it again. The hounds bounded off playfully, racing one another, tongues whipping back as they both fought against one of the wind goddesses.

"Aren't you concerned that the arrows are going to break in their teeth?"

Artemis snorted. "I'm more worried about them slobbering on them."

"Why do it then?"

"It keeps them entertained. The thrill of the hunt, the hum of blood in your veins, the chase, the added hint of danger ... it is not so easy to replicate once you've had a taste of it. You and I both know it. The dogs know it too."

"But the arrows don't harm them. They're already embedded into something by the time the dogs get there," Athena pointed out.

"Ah, but can they catch it before it lands, at the right angle so as not to get hurt?"

"You've trained them to be that fast?"

"Cross-breeding for skill wasn't the stupidest idea the humans came up with. A shame a few of them had to ruin it," Artemis replied.

A tendril of dark hair, the colour of walnut, escaped from her bun and whipped around her face as the wind goddesses came to play amongst the sisters too. Athena and Artemis smiled at one another and let the winds have their fun. It was no use telling them to shoo; they would only persist harder. It was always worth having the elementals on your side as Athena repeatedly told anyone who would listen.

"I have a feeling you didn't ask me all the way here to talk about cross-breeding, dear sister."

"You would be right. But it would be wise for us to wait until the sounds of our words that travel on the winds are only heard by us."

Taking note of her sister's meaning, Artemis released five arrows in immediate succession, directly up into the sky, delighting the wind goddesses and hounds alike with the chaos of it all. Suitably distracted, and moving away with every dance between the arrows and the hounds, Athena spoke quickly.

"We have an issue that requires your assistance, but it is to be kept for your ears only."

Artemis' jaw clenched; like Prometheus, she was known to dislike getting involved in politics. Athena said softly, "It involves a priestess you may have a soft spot for." Artemis' eyes, matching her hair, snapped to hers. "Show me."

....

"I hate to say it, but the she-devil is right."

Artemis referenced Aphrodite once they were back in the war rooms and she'd been briefed, oathed and sworn to secrecy.

"Not words I expected to come out of your mouth," Athena said dryly as she walked to the chaises, retrieved two crystal goblets, and poured wine into them from a small pewter jug that had been left by one of the nymph attendants. Handing Artemis a glass as she retook her seat at the other end of the war table, Athena let her sister continue.

"Not words I often have need to say. But the priestess has left Paris on an instinct humans now call intuition."

"Do you think it's likely that it is tied to her memories here in Olympus?"

Artemis paused. "It is hard to say."

"Prometheus believes they are tied to her instincts, but Aphrodite felt some emotion intertwined with her movements. We are unsure which is driving her at this point. That is why I sought your counsel. You know her true nature best."

"In all likelihood, it is probably both." Artemis told her. "Instinct comes before emotion but emotions can also drive instinct in humans when answered correctly."

"Something I suspect you'd prefer I didn't tell Aphrodite," Athena smiled wryly.

"Quite."

"So you are suggesting we use emotions to drive her instinct to unlock the memories?"

"Amara was always a highly emotional girl. In fact, she was more in tune with the hunt when she listened to her emotions than when she tried to tune them out. So yes, I would say it is your best bet."

"How would you do it?" Athena asked.

"How I originally trained her, like the pups. I would force her into a series of challenges designed to bring out her natural abilities. It's how I became goddess of all that I am. When her back is against the wall, she'll come into her own as I did, albeit she won't be a goddess but her elements are easier to tame than mine were. She can take her training and pass on her knowledge to the rest of the humans. Given you've said you have almost three centuries left, that should be plenty of time for the knowledge to spread and trickle through the bloodlines."

"Do the challenges ever break the pups?"

"One in every twenty pups becomes a quivering mess," Artemis sighed. "But Amara always had a spine of steel. She did, after all, manage to survive in all three of our courts, apparently undetected until now. Young women are braver than we think and stronger than they seem. I say the odds are in her favour. Plus, she agreed to this. She is her own best judge of character. We should trust her to be able to fulfil her moira. And if she fails you, simply come up with a new strategy as you always do."

Athena considered Artemis' words before nodding slowly.

"You are right and your counsel is wise as ever. But what challenges would you suggest we set? There is no Minotaur to slay, and dragons no longer roam the lands. The humans killed all traces of magic, even in the creatures."

"What do the humans fear? Other than themselves?" Artemis asked.

Athena snorted. "Hell. They believe the seven deadly sins will grant them an audience with Dante."

"So use the seven vices."

Athena considered the suggestion. It wasn't a bad idea at all. After all, the Greek gods thrived in that which the human realm now shunned. If there was anything that should penetrate Amara's psyche, it would be an acknowledgement of the old ways. And the seven vices could each serve as a challenge designed to remind her of her alchemy training. If she could find a way to turn each of them to her favour for good, as the gods did, she could complete her task, even if she failed to recall her memories.

Pride, greed, wrath, envy, lust, gluttony, and sloth would each require the help of a different god, goddess, or spirit. The thought of bringing in more people to the deception rubbed like sandpaper against Athena's skin but she could not do this alone. So long as those she roped in didn't know the identity of the priestess, or what she was there for, they might be able to get away with it. Luckily, most ignored Hera's rules anyway and would be happy to help, for it was always fun to meddle in the human world.

"This is all a moot point though," Artemis considered, "until she is exposed to fear in a human body. She must know that intimately first in order to want to fight through the challenges. My pups know it is life and death when they are challenged. The first time I took her through a rite of passage, she believed failure would mean I'd cast her aside and abandonment would kill her. She has to feel that way on Earth. She has to believe it is life or death."

"It is." Athena's usual gleaming eyes held a cloudiness to them.

"How are you going to expose her to the fear?" Artemis asked. "I can't imagine Aphrodite's whiny little son, Phobos of Fear, will do it without his father, and you can't start a war over the girl to get him involved. We don't need a repeat of the Trojan era."

"The Moirai told me to visit them when the challenges arose. As usual, I had no clue what their cryptic words meant until now."

Artemis offered her sister a small smile and a shrug. After all, as Athena well knew, her sister had spent her youth hunting the things down that would solidify her position. These battles that Amara faced would be no different. They would strengthen her in the long run. It would likely hurt though. The Fates were not known for their kindness.

CHAPTER VI

I t was ... rare that the three Fates allowed another god to bear witness to them in person. It happened maybe once a millennium, which was why Athena was not stupid enough to turn it down. They must have something crucial to her success – to the fate of humanity – if they had called her to visit them. Usually they communicated through the cloth, the fabric of the Universe. For Athena, she heard their whispers in the wind. That was how they had laid out the plans to her about the priestess. It had been as clear as listening to a melody.

Long ago, when she had walked amongst the humans, they had told her they never felt the Fates pull around them. They hadn't felt them in their heads or their hearts but in the core of their being. They'd always point to the same place where Prometheus had sealed their beings – the navel. She wondered if Amara now felt the same way.

"I thank you for the audience, Moirai."

Of course, the three Fates seated round the fireplace that warmed Athena's back were not of their own appearance. Instead they had disguised themselves as ancient crones, each with swamps of cloth in black, white, and green to hide their bodies, and hoods that covered most of their features. All Athena could see were gnarled old hands with long talon-like claws peeking out from sleeves, and wrinkles on faces that were so plentiful they caused the skin to sag. Nothing like what they were rumoured to look like ... but then, no one – god or human – could say for certain who had seen the Fates' true faces.

She was grateful for the fire. The room to which they'd summoned her, after she had sent word to them, was bare and draughty. There was only a rug underneath her feet, of ruby reds and diamond blues in a pattern Athena recognised as eighteenth century. The rest of the furniture, the pieces the Moirai weren't sitting on, was covered in white sheets. It was not that the draught concerned Athena but the presence of the Moirai. It was as if they seeped the life, the warmth, the depth, out of everything around them to use it for the purpose of weaving the story of life itself. Athena shuddered, a wave of pins and needles travelling up her spine.

"You need help with the priestess," the middle one astutely calculated, her voice so crystal clear it hurt Athena's ears to hear it and she winced ever so slightly. The Moirai's eyes watched her, calculating.

"Yes. There was an unseen complication," Athena carefully replied.

"Ah but that has always been your downfall has it not, Athena? Your inability to be foolproof." Lachesis continued.

The Moirai cackled as Athena clenched her jaw. It was the cruellest paradox they had burdened upon her, and now they openly mocked her for it. For all her wisdom, all her experience, knowledge, and sound judgement, the actions on the battlefield could not always be predicted. It was in those moments, where new precedents were set, where the unexpected happened, that Athena's wisdom was useless. And who would trust the Goddess of Wisdom and War if she revealed that she could not know which consequences would arise from her actions? It mattered little that, when it came to war, there was no such thing as a foolproof strategy, that each move was calculated based on how the defence responded. In Olympus, reputation counted for everything.

She got the distinct impression she was being toyed with, as a cat might play with a mouse, but she allowed her anger to froth, like a wave breaking against the surface of her skin, and then simmer inside of her. To waste such an opportunity for the Moirai's help would do no good now.

"It would appear the priestess we were planning on using to execute my plan has lost her memories."

"We know, foolish girl," the middle one waved her hand and Athena heard bones crackle, though she was standing a metre away. Never had she been called a girl in her life, much less a foolish one. The smart stung as if she'd been slapped on the cheek.

"You asked that she be left alone when we placed her on Earth ..."

"We know what we asked," the first of the three and closest to Athena said. Her black cloak looked mauve when she angled her head slightly and the light coming through the window behind them hit it. "The fear of abandonment will serve her."

Athena waited patiently for the Moirai to elaborate but received nothing further. Her teeth clenched together impossibly tighter.

"Without her memories, we have little chance of her using her alchemy skills in the human realm." Athena ground out, surprising herself with how calm she sounded when the frustration was already beginning to build in her again like a crescendo. She would not ask for an audience with the Moirai again for at least a millenium she told herself.

"You ask for a boon," the third sister said, shifting her weight in the chair. Her elbows balanced on the arms of it precariously as she leant forward in anticipation. The shape of the cloth she wore, they all wore, fell into lines and shadows that told Athena their bones were thin, old if the cracking was anything to go by, but she doubted they would ever break. No one could break the Moirai to their will, only barter and hope the fickle sisters were in a whimsical enough mood to hear their plea.

"We need her to be introduced to fear. You are the ones who ultimately determine who is exposed to what, so I come to you."

When they didn't respond, Athena muttered darkly, "Yes, I ask for a boon."

Two of the sisters turned their hooded heads to the figure on the left of Athena, the one closest to her, who in turn lifted her chin enough that Athena could see the whites of her eyes beneath her hood.

"It will come at great cost," the first sister whispered silkily, "for there is no other way. To pull from a thread that is unwilling, you must take from another."

Athena waited patiently for further explanation again. This time, to her surprise, she received it.

"The fear will claw at her more savagely than if it had passed through her life naturally. You will watch her contort in horror, in pain, in revulsion as it takes root. Until her eyes go blank and she retreats into the shell of her mind for safe harbour. She will wrap shame, embroidered with fear, around her skin as a blanket. All this you shall bear witness to. Are you sure this is a boon you are willing to ask for?"

Three heads cocked as they watched her. Three mouths smiled cruelly at her in her predicament. Six hands curled over chair arms as they anticipated her response.

Athena closed her eyes and took a deep breath.

"Will it save them? The humans?" she asked quietly. For she did not want to see thousands of years of work wasted. She too had come to view the humans as precious, as something of note for the gods, even if those in Olympus couldn't see what good having the humans did for them beyond stroke their egos. If that meant she had to put her priestess through hardship, so be it. Others she had watched over in her time – Hercules, Jason – had survived. Amara could too.

"Certainly," the first of the Fates replied without pause.

"And there is no other boon you are willing to offer?" She had to try, for every fibre of her being was screaming that the Moirai were being deliberately obtuse, that she would regret the cost of this decision, that it would haunt her for eternity. Paradoxically, she knew she would still do it because she knew the answer before it came out of their crooked mouths.

"It is the only way."

A pause, the weight of Athena's words heavy on her armoured chest as she spoke them.

"Then yes, it is the boon I ask for."

CHAPTER VII

"The best adventures come with a little risk."

It was that thought that Amara held in her mind as she made her way across the Channel and landed in England at St Pancras station to be met with a barrage of assaults on her senses. Trains whistled over the constant chatter of commuters on their phones, and heavy, impatient feet slammed against concrete. Shoulders barged past her as they moved through the swarm of passengers on the platform. Everywhere she looked, heads bobbed along, working their way to the end of the platform. The smell of colognes and perfumes mixed with sweat, and vendors offering fresh food, made for an unpleasant combination of notes that tantalised even as it repulsed Amara. Even the air felt dense, heavy, difficult to breathe through.

She had an hour to wait until her connecting train took her on to Edinburgh. As she was desperately hungry, she went in search of the nearest eatery. After spending an entire day's worth of money she'd set aside for herself on one tiny meal – a "homemade" BLT that had been soggy and cold and a coffee that had no depth of flavour – she was glad to not be staying in London. It was a strange city that reminded her of home and yet didn't. It was unfriendly like most big cities yet unpleasant, she decided. Paying the bill by pulling out a couple of crisp notes from the rolled-up wad that had been buried deep in her tan leather bag that she slung across her chest as she stood, Amara headed back towards the station to catch her train to Edinburgh.

The train this time wasn't as packed as it had been for her journey from Paris to London. The royal blue seats were plush to the eye, though not so much to the bum. She wriggled slightly, trying to adjust into a position that took maximum advantage of the limited padding in her seat. When she was comfortable, Amara looked around and saw that the carriage was occupied with three others and herself, though it had space for at least fifty. She'd chosen the carriage near the front of the train for its proximity to the toilet. According to the train guard that had just come over the intercom, she could expect a trolley service shortly too. Had she known that, she might not have ordered that pathetic sandwich.

As the train began to pull away, Amara felt a tugging sensation within her snap. As if she'd just done something that could not be undone, or some twist of fate had painfully bound itself into place. Her spine locked, but as the train continued to roll out across the English capital and beyond into the countryside, she finally let the rhythm of the train soothe her senses.

It wasn't until two hours into the journey that Amara's eyes focused on the scenery in front of her, that she began to notice the man in the window staring at her. Examining the reflection, she could see that he had a round face, with ears that protruded slightly from underneath a mop of dirty blonde curls. His nose was curved and narrow, as if the smell in the carriage already offended him, and his eyes were as cat-like in shape as her own. Those eyes were definitely watching her.

She couldn't tell much else so she yawned, stretched her arms above her head, and resettled her gaze towards the carriage as if just making herself comfortable.

He was still staring.

Gaze lowered, Amara could still feel his eyes burrowing into her before she realised, as he came into her periphery, that he'd decided to be bold enough to stand up and come towards her.

"I'm terribly sorry, lassie. Do you mind if I sit here?"

His accent sounded almost Gaelic, the words rolling around and out of his mouth in a rhythmic nature that Amara found warm and pleasant, even as his ice-blue eyes bored holes into her.

"Not at all," Amara replied, gesturing to the seat in front of her, the table providing some barrier of protection from this stranger who seemed far too interested in her. For what else could she do? Say no? With what God-given reason?

"You heading to Edinburgh?"

Given that was the only destination for the train, Amara thought it was a bit of a redundant question, but perhaps the man was just being polite in his small talk. She hated making people feel uncomfortable and so, while she would have preferred to stay in silence, she answered him.

"Yes, you?"

"Aye, back home to see the little sister and her wee ones."

"Oh, that's nice."

"What about you?"

"Excuse me?"

"Why are you heading to Edinburgh? If you don't mind me asking ..." He smiled a lopsided grin that made him look charming and defenceless, and Amara silently berated herself again for being so defensive.

She shrugged. "Felt like exploring the country."

"Ah an explorer, aye. I could tell you weren't from around these parts."

"What do you mean?" she asked, a curious smile on her lips, but already her stomach was free falling. What if she wasn't wanted in Edinburgh? The thought, unwanted, crept into her mind.

"I don't mean to be rude, mind, it's just we don't see many folks of your ... *complexion* back home. Most of us are pasty white redheads." He laughed, like her skin colour was a matter of how many hours she spent in the sun. Suddenly, she didn't feel quite so bad about making him feel uncomfortable and threw him a stony look.

He held his hands up. "I didn't mean any offence. I'm just trying to be honest with ya. There'll be some folk back home who will be less accommodating."

Unlike you, an honest racist, she thought to herself, though it must have been written as clear across her face as newspaper ink.

"I'm sorry, I've offended ya. I can see that."

When Amara continued to ignore him in favour of staring out the window, he slid a can of lager across the table between them. When Amara stared at it poisonously, he said, "It's a peace offering. It won't kill ya."

Amara stared at the can. She didn't want it, but the man across from her was still staring and she was becoming more uncomfortable with every passing second.

"Go on," he encouraged.

The need to prove a point bowed to the need to stop the uncomfortable stare of this stranger. Amara slowly took the can, tapped on the top, and opened it to a hiss. Raising it to her lips she kept her eyes on the stranger across from her and took a small sip, ashamed of herself for caving. It tasted like cat piss, but she swallowed it anyway. It was better than the conversation.

"I'm Ralph," the stranger said, reaching his hand across the table.

"Amara," she answered, returning the gesture in kind because she felt she had to, now that she had accepted a gift from him, even as she tried to sink deeper back into her seat.

"Ya know, you remind me of someone."

"I do?" she asked, not particularly interested.

"Yeah, a woman I knew. Long time ago now. She looked at me like you're looking at me now when she first met me." Ralph pulled such a boyish scowl that Amara couldn't help it, she laughed out loud.

"Aye, she did that too. Laughed like there wasn't a care in the world. Usually because I'd done something daft." He shrugged in a self-deprecating sort of way. He smiled, except the smile wasn't for Amara this time. It was for the lady in his thoughts. One that put that far away look on his face. Amara felt her defences melting ever so slightly.

"When she laughed, it was like all she needed was the breath in her lungs and she'd have a life worth living," he continued.

"That's beautiful." Amara replied, caught off guard by his words.

"Aye, her words not mine. I ain't no poet." He shrugged and took a swig from his can of lager.

And so that was how Amara and Ralph spent the rest of the trip to Edinburgh, sipping lager and making small talk about times past.

"Wow, this place is ... wow." Amara breathed, trying to take it all in.

Ralph eyed her. "Alright, you'd think you'd never seen a train station before."

"Not one that looks like this."

Where the glass dome made it feel like she was walking through a cathedral and the teal marble tiles gave Amara the impression she was gliding across water. Even the shops surrounding the main area of the station and the fast-food joint didn't detract from the sense that she had just stepped through a portal fit for ... royalty. She wasn't royalty, but the calming breath that filled her lungs whispered one word.

Home.

A twinge of knowledge whispered in Amara's ear but, as quickly as she became aware of it, it floated out of her head again. She knew after years of experience, grasping at the whisper would do no good. It would come back when she needed it.

"Are your sister and her kids here?" she asked Ralph, who was still standing beside her, a cargo green army bag slung over his shoulder.

He was shorter than Amara had realised when he was sitting opposite her, maybe only a couple of inches taller than her at best, though she was tall at five-foot nine. He wasn't overly stocky either. Just an average height and average build for an average man, she supposed. He'd been good company on the trip though, apart from that initial faux pax, and kept her entertained with stories of what she could expect in Edinburgh.

"Nah, I'll just hop in a taxi and head over to surprise 'em. Don't suppose you know where you're going?"

Amara pulled what she hoped was an 'easy-go-lucky' traveller's smile.

"No, but I'm sure I'll figure it out."

"Aye, why don't you come with me? Just for a hot meal, like. Ain't no hostel going to be serving food at this hour and you don't want to eat alone. Plus, if you have a few drinks, you can have the spare room. I'll crash on the sofa. I know ma sis won't mind."

"Oh no, I couldn't."

83

"Nah, come on. I insist. Give yourself a chance to get a hot meal in your belly and find your footing before exploring our beautiful hometown."

"I wouldn't want to impose though ..."

"You won't be imposing. Come on, I won't take no for an answer now I've thought about it a lil'."

Amara hesitated and he saw it, taking it as good as a yes, and practically ushered her out of the station, one pudgy, sweaty hand on her lower back.

It turned out his sister didn't live too far away at all. Then again, from what Amara could tell from the taxi window, Edinburgh didn't seem that big. Oh but it was beautiful though, even if they'd arrived on a cold, wet evening that promised this winter would be cruel. It was all the more dramatic for being lit up against shiny, wet pavements. The castle sitting on the top of the hill overlooked the city, an imposing draconian building that watched over tiny humans going about their business in the dark. The gothic architecture of the buildings, lit from within, cast dark shadows across the streets. Amara watched from the taxi window as people scuttled along the streets. The city was alive with the hum of activity that said this was a healthy population who felt safe with one another, even in the darkest of night. That was Amara's first impression of Edinburgh.

It was not to be her second.

Pulling up at the end of a set of terraced houses several minutes later, Amara and Ralph thanked the taxi driver as they got out. Amara turned and stared at the small house in front of them. It certainly didn't look like the four-bedroom terraced house her travelling companion had described. The light above the door showed that the iron black gate wasn't rusty and the garden bushes were neatly trimmed. Even with little light, she could tell it was a house that was loved and well taken care of. Not what Amara was expecting from a single mother raising three children alone. She'd half expected abandoned bikes and toys strewn about, weeds sprouting where they could.

She internally scolded herself for her prejudice.

Opening the gate, which protested with a high-pitched squeal at its unoiled hinges that echoed across the otherwise empty road, Ralph only had to take three steps before he could knock on the door. He ushered for Amara to come stand beside him.

The hallway light flickered on and the door opened a moment later to reveal a woman in her mid-thirties at best, with strawberry blonde hair that neatly bounced around her shoulders. She wore a white button-up top with sleeves rolled up, revealing her lightly freckled arms under the glow of the light and dark-green cargo capris which were held tightly to her small frame with a simple brown leather belt and brass buckle. She was much more petite than Amara had imagined, but when she saw who was at the door, the scowl on her face became mighty large.

"What the HELL are you doing here, Ralph?!" she hissed in a furious whisper.

"Hey sis, good to see you too."

The scowl deepened. Ralph's sister kept one arm on the door, the other on the doorframe, blocking the entrance with her body.

"I told you I never wanted you to turn up on my doorstep again. And who the hell is this?"

The woman in the doorway pointed straight at Amara.

"This," the Scotsman said, pushing Amara in between them, "is a friend of mine, who needs a hot meal and a place to stay for the night."

"Oh no I—" Amara began, but Ralph spoke over her loudly, apparently uncaring about waking up the neighbours.

"She's never been to Edinburgh before. Would you really be the one to turn her away when I've told her so much about our proud hospitality? Would you see her sleep on the street?"

"I have a good mind to turn you away alright," his sister scowled. She turned her assessing gaze to Amara, giving her the once over. As per usual with strangers, Amara felt their tension and automatically tried to soothe it by calming her own rapid heartbeat. Ralph's sister did what all the others in the past had done, which was to take a deep breath and allow her shoulders to drop. Surmising Amara wasn't a threat and nodding to herself, she gestured for Amara to walk past her before she slammed her arm back across the door jamb.

"Just this one night. I mean it, Ralph."

"Ah you're a good egg, Liss."

"I'm a fool who can't bear to think of people on the street is what I am," she muttered as Ralph followed Amara down the thin corridor and into the illuminated kitchen at the end of it.

True to her brother's word, Liss was an impeccable host. Her home was beautifully kept. While Amara had only been shown the kitchen and the spare room to place her bag down, it was enough to tell her exactly how proud this woman was of her home. Amara immediately liked her.

The kitchen itself was small with a light, round wooden table that had been sanded back to the grain, and four chairs, sitting smack bang in the middle of it. The fridge was to the right of the table and the countertops made their way from the fridge around the room in an L shape with plenty of white cupboards above them, apart from a window above the sink countertop. It would mean Liss would have her back to the table if she was washing dishes but at least she probably had a lovely view of her back garden during the day. The blind above the window was white with blue waves decorating the edges, which matched the table placemats and coasters. All the dishes were drying neatly on the white plastic rack beside the sink and there was nothing on the countertops that was out of place. Even the eggshell-blue microwave, kettle, and toaster looked artfully placed.

"This is all I have I'm afraid," Liss said as she placed two large bowls of heated-up beef stew and potato dumplings in front of Amara and Ralph, accompanied with cans of lager, identical to the ones they had been drinking on the train together.

"It was supposed to see me and the kids through till tomorrow. Guess I'll have to go to the shops in the morning instead," she muttered.

"We're sorry for putting you out," Amara said, though Ralph had already scooped his spoon deep in the bowl and had his mouth full, not looking apologetic in the slightest.

"Ah nothing for you to apologise for, love." Liss sent a daggered stare at her brother, who continued – willingly or not – to be oblivious. Amara squirmed in her seat.

"Perhaps I should leave you two to catch up?" she offered.

"No. Stay. Eat. I need to go make up the spare bed for you," Liss said.

"I'll sleep on the sofa, Liss. Give our guest the good bed." Ralph grinned that lopsided grin of his and Amara settled on the impression that he was being deliberately obtuse.

Liss said nothing directly but muttered something under her breath about "our guest alright," before heading out of the small kitchen, back into the hallway, and up the stairs on the right to make up the extra bed. Quietly, of course. She'd already told them – more specifically, a loud Ralph – to keep it down as all the little ones were asleep.

When Amara was sure she was out of earshot, she finally looked at her train companion.

"So, your sister didn't know you were coming."

"Aye, I was coming to make amends." At least now he had the decency to look sheepish.

"And you thought to use me as ... a bargaining chip?" Amara scrunched up her nose.

"Nah, not at all. I just, well, it's always easier when there's a buffer there, ya know? And yeah, I saw an opportunity. But I'm not sorry I took it. Can you really tell me you are?"

Amara went to argue then closed her mouth again. She couldn't exactly disagree. Given how much the meal in London had cost her, and the train fare, being given a free meal and roof over her head for the first night in a new city had certainly been welcome, not least to her wad of cash tucked away upstairs with her belongings.

"Still, I don't like being used."

"Aye, I get that. I'm sorry, truly I am."

Amara said nothing to that, her focus on the food in front of her. She spooned broth into her mouth and restrained herself from sighing. She didn't want Ralph to feel like her contentment had anything to do with him. Gratitude and annoyance battled inside of her for space. Annoyance clearly won out and set a scowl across her face.

"Some would call me an asshole for needing to ask for your forgiveness twice in such a short space of time," Ralph said, noticing her expression and slightly slurring his words now. It had been a long day with a lot of lager.

"Some would," Amara agreed.

"I shouldn't even ask. I'm a terrible human being," he muttered.

Amara looked at him, but his head was now bent into his hands. She sighed. She didn't want to be responsible for his mood. He clearly had enough demons clinging to his shoulders if he had problems with his sister and, clearly, with alcohol. She reached across and grabbed one of his hands.

"It's ok ... I get it. Truly I do."

"I just wanted to see my lil' sister again." Ralph hiccupped.

"I know, and you've both been kind and generous to me. I won't be one to hold a grudge."

"Thanks." Ralph hiccupped again.

They were finishing their meals as his sister walked back in.

"The bed's ready for you whenever you are, hen." Liss took a seat opposite them, her back to the window.

"On that note, I'll leave you two to catch up." Amara thanked her hosts graciously, and after fussing with Liss about who would clean the dishes, moved upstairs to the room where she'd placed her bags earlier.

It wasn't until a few hours later, when Amara's bladder protested, that she heard whispers from the landing.

"... you turned up here battered and bruised, hollering that you were going to break the door down! You scared the kids half to death! Of course I weren't joking about you never coming back here!"

"Ah the kids are fine, aren't they?"

"No thanks to you! What the hell were you thinking bringing ..."

"Ah, psh! We heard much worse growing up. Stop your moaning."

"Moaning? Moaning?! Look at you! You turned out just like Da."

"And look what it turned you into, you s-st-stuck up bitch."

Amara gasped. There was a slur to the words but they were no less snide for it.

"First Ma then Mary, now you. Don't know how to handle a real man, so you toss them aside ... innt that right?"

"Don't you do that. Don't you dare. Not under my roof. I won't have it, you hear me?" Liss hissed. "Don't you project all your Mary crap onto me. I didn't hurt ya. I didn't abandon ya. I didn't sleep with your best friend! I just asked ya not to show up here slaughtered, and now look at ya. I knew I shouldn't have taken you in tonight, but where else are you going to go? You've burnt bridges with everyone in town. No one would have you. I only do it because you're blood and if I turned you away, Ma would turn in her grave."

"I don't have to stand here 'n listen to this b-bul-bullshit."

"No that's right, you go on and drink some more. Leave that poor lil' lassie here. Go and get yourself shitfaced and don't bother calling me when you end up in some coppers van 'cause you threatened the next guy who looked at you funny."

A burp, a brief pause, footsteps, and a slammed door.

"Goddamn it."

Amara decided to go back to bed unnoticed.

When she awoke again, the stench of Scotch and stale lager invaded her nose to the point her eyes began to blink back tears. Rubbing the sleep from her eyes, she felt her hand brush against something before that something clasped at her wrist and pinned it above her head. Another hand slammed over her mouth as her eyes flew open.

"Shh, shh ... I'm not here to hurt you," Ralph crooned, releasing the hand over her mouth as he did so.

"Ralph, how did you get in? Why are you ..."

"Shh," he continued, stroking the back of his hand down the side of her cheek.

Amara found herself unable to do anything, her body wouldn't move, her mind kept drawing a blank. Only her eyes raced back and forth over his, trying to figure out what his actions meant, what he was doing.

"You're going to be just like her," he said sadly, looking at her with forlorn eyes before curling his hands in her hair that had worked its way loose in the plait she'd put it in before bed.

"Ralph, what are you talking about?!"

"You're going to leave me."

"Ralph, you're drunk. I—"

"I won't let you leave me again, Ma-Mara-Mary. I won't. I'll give it to you like a real man. I'll show ya ..."

Finally Amara's brain kicked in and her legs lashed out. Too late. She realised he already had one leg between both of hers. He pinned her arms down, tugging off only as much of the duvet as he needed to, pushed her legs further apart, her wrists now both caught in a bruising grip as his mouth slammed over hers to muffle her scream, and his other hand began to touch her ... callously, cruelly. Then it wasn't his hand.

It hurt.

CHAPTER VIII

Amara spent the following three months wandering around Edinburgh blindly. Luckily, the weather drove most inside, so the narrow pavements had unexpected ample space. But when she did encounter people, she found them interfering and problematic, stepping into her way where she walked, encroaching or just *right* behind her in a way that set her teeth on edge. She caught snippets of conversations between strangers as they passed her on the street, but she didn't engage in conversations herself. She didn't look up, she didn't smile, she didn't make eye contact.

When someone, a man with dark hair and spectacles, appeared at the opposite end of the alleyway Amara found herself in, her heart began to ricochet in her chest. She could have sworn it was loud enough for him to hear even from thirty feet away. She hunched her shoulders and turned back the way she came. Her footsteps quickened but so did his, the echoes snapping at her heels. Her hands were shaking and she stuffed them deep in her pockets so he couldn't know how frightened she was as she almost broke into a light jog. Amara didn't even realise she was holding her breath until she exited the alley onto an open street and dragged deep lungfuls of air into her. The man exited several seconds later, shot her a concerned look, and strode off in the opposite direction. She didn't walk through the alleyways that seventeenth-century drunks would have been dragged behind and killed after that.

One day she found herself on a mosaic where a quick search on her phone told her she was standing on the exact spot they used to hang murderers, rapists, and witches. She turned in a full circle, staring at the mosaic, absorbing every element of it, expecting to feel something … anything. Anger, rage, grief. Instead she felt nothing, her mind empty and her bones cold. Oh so achingly cold. Not even the brightly painted shops, the food delicacies she would have savoured, or the trinkets she would have treasured could warm her. She wrapped her red wool coat tighter to her body, crossing her arms and stuffing her gloved hands under her armpits as she continued walking, with no place to go.

At night, fear moved skittishly in the shadows that fell from the gothic buildings above her. Surrounding her. Overshadowing her. The butterflies in her stomach she'd had from the sense of adventure when she'd first arrived had turned acidic, each nervous wingbeat making her stomach revolt. The butterflies had revealed themselves to be moths with fangs that sunk their venom into her skin, turning the acid in her stomach putrid and violent until it gorged on itself, churning convulsively until it rose from her mouth and directly into the nearest receptacle.

So before night fell, Amara was holed up, alone, in her cheap hotel room off Princes Street. Always alone.

She had no idea what she was still doing here, why she didn't just get on the first train back to Paris, back home. The thought of the train station always stopped her. What if he was there again? What if she bumped into him? She knew it was an irrational thought. It didn't matter that there were over half a million people in the city. It didn't matter that she was just as likely to bump into him on the street as she was there. They had been there together, and her mind wouldn't let her forget it. She couldn't stop thinking about it.

She would fall asleep and dream of the train station. And there he was, in the middle of it, just standing there, watching her. The colours around them would drain as the smile she had once thought of as harmless turned into a cruel sneer. And always she'd wake in sweat-soaked sheets tangled around her.

She couldn't go back. She should never have left in the first place. She'd been rash and foolish and someone should have stopped her. Father Michel should have stopped her, if he ever really cared about her. Even her memory was starting to doubt her on that. What was it about her that made people not care? Why had Ralph not cared? Father Michel? Her mother who abandoned her? What was it about her?

Night after night, on crisp but firm white sheets that reminded her thirty pounds a night only went so far, and savings that were supposed to last her six months rapidly disappearing, she went over in her head what she could have done differently that night. What she *should* have done differently.

Fear and doubt were the only ones that cared about her now, her mind whispered. All they demanded was payment. Attention. In turn, they told her all the things she had to fix and change about herself to make others care, to make sure she wasn't abandoned, unwanted, disposed of ... again. So she listened to them and she paid her dues. Every time she got close to an answer, doubt would whisper in her ear that she couldn't be trusted. And so the answer slipped away again.

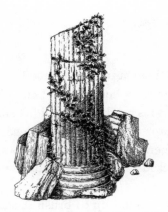

CHAPTER IX

A phrodite was fuming.

She had watched the priestess become overpowered by that pathetic excuse for a human man, had watched that disgusting act with rage boiling beneath her bones and felt her ichor run cold. That was no way to treat one of her priestesses. To do so was a stain on her honour, the act not only repugnant but an obvious mockery of all that Aphrodite held sacred.

She couldn't believe Athena would have ordered it, civilized and protective as she was. Even Artemis, for all her wild ways surely wouldn't have suggested ... *that*. They were both virgins. Surely they would not have willingly let that title be stripped from Amara. There were, after all, other ways to evoke fear in a woman. As the thought passed through her head, she wondered if her sisters' chastity had blinded them to that fact. It hadn't even *worked*. Three months later and the priestess was still no closer to accessing her alchemy.

Aphrodite's thoughts abruptly cut off at the sight of the man striding towards her. His wild curls had now been shaved closely to his head, but that didn't stop him looking any less feral. Bronzed muscles that bulged, fighting to get out of his leathers, moved languidly towards her. Dark brown eyes tracked her, like prey, until they were standing toe to toe.

She reached a hand up to brush it against his hair, but he captured her delicate wrist, spun her around and had her pinned to the wall, her wrist above her head and a rock-solid, thick thigh pushed between the pair of hers between one breath and the next. She felt warmth invade her as he overwhelmed every inch of her personal space, the cologne of sweat and frankincense, a sweetness that reminded her of their many stolen nights together. It was all consuming and she forgot what had turned her heart cold only moments ago.

"Ares," she said softly.

"My love," he growled. She knew it wasn't in anger. Always so angry, her Ares, but never with her. It was something deeper, richer, more passionate when it was just the two of them. His growl ignited a low heat that started in her belly and spread ... everywhere. Before she could ask him what he was doing here, he gripped her hair, his hands adorned with assorted metal rings, and pulled her in for a kiss of duelling tongues and teeth until she pushed at his wide chest and gasped for breath.

"I've missed you, lover," he said darkly.

"I've missed you too," she replied, petting his chest until she could hear his chest rumble in agreement. He was like a large mountain lion, easy to pet if he decided he wasn't going to eat you. Although ... when he had the appetite ... Aphrodite sighed in nostalgia as her thighs clenched involuntarily and she remembered why she was in the open-aired corridor that led to Athena's war rooms.

"Let me down, Ares, my love. I must speak to Athena."

Immediately he released his hold in her hair and on her wrist, removing his thigh in a swift move. But his eyes, they kept her pinned to the stone wall.

"I must speak with her too – boring battle plans." He shrugged, heaving shoulders the size of rocks as if the weight of him was nothing. He was a magnificent man, but while his body would usually seduce her, his words were enough of a nudge to switch mercurial Aphrodite from her temptress thoughts to ones more pristine in nature. She had come here because her priestess had undergone a rape, a direct violation of all Aphrodite stood for, in the name of Athena's greater plan for humanity. Rearranging her pleated sky-blue skirt around her legs and smoothing hair of the purest white, Aphrodite composed herself from the dishevelled look she always seemed to develop in a heartbeat when she and Ares managed to find themselves truly alone for a moment.

"Yes, well, me first."

"Always," Ares smirked.

At that precise moment, Athena swung open the great wooden doors, which were etched with carvings of her most treasured victories in history.

"Ares, there you are. And Aphrodite. Well, well, well, have you two been up to old tricks again?"

Aphrodite's smile was saccharine with an undertone of seething hatred.

"No, but apparently you have, dear sister."

With her skirt pleats dancing around her, Aphrodite stormed past Athena into her war rooms. Ares followed, somewhat less theatrically. Not waiting until the door was closed, Aphrodite whipped round and immediately sent a volley of insults in Greek, Latin, Arabic, and French. Even Ares, bullish as he was, blushed at some of the names she called Athena.

"Are you done?"

Aphrodite, pursed lips painted blood red, took a breath and replied calmly.

"Yes, I think that covers it."

"Now," said Athena, who still stood by the doorway, arms crossed, "would you care to explain why you just verbally accosted me?"

Aphrodite cocked her head to the side and stared, hard at her.

"I'll answer your question with one of my own. What did Artemis have to say for herself when the pair of you discussed Amara?"

Athena arched an eyebrow and uttered a dry laugh. "She actually agreed with you about the fear."

Aphrodite's eyes narrowed to slits before she smiled coyly. "And pray tell, how did you go about instilling fear in the girl?" While the smile remained, her tone cut like shards of glass and Athena got the sinking feeling she was about to be told disastrous news.

"I handled it," she replied smoothly, her fingers drumming on the war table.

"Did you now?"

Athena was no fool. She knew the words the Moirai had told her of the boon off by heart and there was only one reason Aphrodite would be here in this state. That she had sanctioned the act that had undoubtedly brought Aphrodite to her chambers, unknowingly or not, made bile burn the back of her throat but she could not show weakness now. Not in front of Aphrodite and certainly not in front of Ares, who was watching the two sisters as a lion watches gazelles when he isn't hungry, positively bored yet under no pretence should you think he was sleeping. In reality, she knew he was simply observing with as little energy as required, unless Aphrodite went to gouge out her eyes and there was actual bloodshed. In which case, Athena had no doubt her brother would help his beloved if only so he could claim to be the only Olympic god to be associated with warfare should they destroy her.

"We did what was necessary to protect the humans."

"What you did WAS. NOT. PROTECTION!"

For a minute, the mask dropped and the ugly veneer of Aphrodite, the vicious she-devil that lurked beneath, came forward, all teeth and snarls, her face contorted in a way that didn't befit her image. It was not the first time Athena or Ares had seen this face. It was, however, a mark of how pissed off Aphrodite was. Cerberus, the multi-headed dog who guarded the underworld for Hades, looked tame in comparison.

"It was a necessary loss to win the war," Athena said quietly.

Aphrodite laughed now but her usual tinkle was replaced with something darker, something much more venomous. "A loss is an inept word for what you put that girl through."

Athena physically flinched as she took the blow.

"How *could* you?! How could you even *ask* that of one of your priestesses? I would *never* even question asking that of mine. She *was* one of mine!"

"Amara knew the cost of battle. She knew exactly what she was getting herself into." Athena's steely resolve threatened to crack but she couldn't give away her secret, her shame at not knowing the thread the Moirai would pull. Everyone on board with this plan had to believe Athena knew what she was doing even if they hated her for it, or they wouldn't trust her wisdom and follow through when she needed them to.

"Oh did she?"

Athena didn't answer, locking her jaw and staring at Aphrodite defiantly. If she had to take the lashing from Aphrodite, so be it.

"No, she didn't. How could she? How could a priestess from our world ever know the true span of human emotions? How everything they feel is heightened to the nth degree? Pleasure, pain, grief, regret, shame? You may have breathed life into them, but I'm the one that gifted Prometheus with their emotional intellect, Athena. Or have you forgotten?"

Athena remained silent.

"You have damned that girl for eternity. She will never get back what you allowed to be stolen."

"She will heal."

"Oh and you know that how, oh virtuous one with your virginity intact? You who knows nothing of the carnal pleasures of sex or the vulnerability of making love? How do you know she will heal from something you know *nothing* about?!"

"Where you see ruin in the rubble, I see glory." Athena said.

Aphrodite snorted. "I think Dionysus has been spiking your victory drinks, sister."

"You may not see it, but because of this, she will rise. Stronger, smarter, wiser. She will lead them through the fear that chokes them."

"Your wisdom is heartless."

A deep rumbling cough interrupted them.

"If I may," Ares interjected, "Athena is right in one instance."

Aphrodite stared at him as if he'd just presented her with a rotten trout. Athena, too, was surprised. She had never known Ares to disagree with his lover in public.

"In the heat of battle, it's the hardship, the urge not to be defeated that will keep this priestess of yours going."

Before Aphrodite could rebuke him, Ares continued.

"But Athena has made one, perhaps critical, mistake."

Athena scoffed. Ares was not usually one to make any plans, let alone analyse others and point out flaws in them.

"She has forgotten that love," his eyes stared unblinking at Aphrodite, "is as relentless, remorseless, and ruthless as she is in her pursuit for justice. I fear, Athena, you may have made an enemy in this battle that could cost you the war."

Aphrodite smiled savagely.

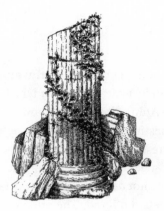

CHAPTER X

S he may not have her sister's head for strategy but Aphrodite was no idiot. She sunk back into the bathtub with a sigh. The cream marble with gold trim was embedded into the rock of the room at waist length in the shape of a conch shell. It was deep enough that the base of it was level with the floor, which is why it required three steps to climb in and sink into its depths. Inside the bath, there were seated edges if one preferred not to float.

Aphrodite liked to float. Surrounded as she was with rose petals and myrtles that kissed her skin before floating away allowed her to think better. Her long hair, water clogged, gave the impression that she was haloed should anyone look upon her, while her full breasts and pearl-pink nipples broke the surface of the otherwise crystalline water. Alas, Ares had gone off to do some such task – Aphrodite hadn't cared to ask what – and she'd headed back to her rooms to draw a scalding hot bath to think. She was well and truly alone with her thoughts and one pressing conundrum.

She knew how to play with powerful immortals. Athena was no exception just because she had the head for war and wisdom. While Aphrodite knew Artemis – given her pride over her own chastity – would be equally as enraged to learn about the priestess' virginity being stripped from her, they still weren't on speaking terms. Roping her in to help with this problem was not an option. Ares was far too bullish to help, though he had offered. The others who knew of the plan had been recruited by Athena and paid handsomely for it. All Aphrodite could offer those gods that Athena could not was a night in her bed chambers, and she didn't feel that whoring herself out in exchange for their cooperation would particularly send the right message. Which left ... Prometheus.

Aphrodite sighed, reaching for the rose oil which she rubbed up and down her legs before resubmerging them in the water. She would have to make amends.

"Hermes."

Immediately the old god – though 'old' was a relative term given that he was one of the youngest of all the Olympians – appeared before her. With walnut-coloured skin, he still had the youthful confidence of a young boy that had just blossomed into a well-endowed young man Aphrodite noted while she blatantly perused her old lover's body.

"Aphrodite." Hermes smiled and it was a warm smile, of summer evenings spent together sipping wine with a god who was comfortable in his skin and sexuality and asked no more of Aphrodite then she was willing to give. Indeed, he had been one of her favourite lovers for his ability to know when to give and when to take. It was, she realised, what made him such a wonderful negotiator.

"I need you to get a message to Prometheus."

Hermes' eyebrow quirked into a curve.

"It's not what you think," she admonished coyly.

"I think you have the look of a woman intent on getting her way."

Aphrodite laughed. "Perhaps you *do* know me better than I thought."

It had taken Hermes some cajoling on his part to get her into bed the first time, though he had soon proved his skill. Memories of how playful they were together spilled into her mind and Aphrodite found herself wanting to re-experience him.

As if reading her thoughts, Hermes took a seat on the edge of the bathtub, his fingertips gently skimming the water, creating ripples that traced all the way back to Aphrodite's breasts.

Butterflies erupted into symphony and Aphrodite decided that perhaps a release was exactly what she needed before sending a message to Prometheus. Perhaps if she were in a less frustrated mood, he'd be more receptive to her message, she reasoned.

"Would you like to join me first?" she asked the god, who watched her with dark caramel eyes flecked with gold.

"I thought you'd never ask."

Prometheus was not quite so forthcoming.

"What is it that you want, Aphrodite?" he growled, prowling around the fountain in the courtyard outside her rooms, where she had requested an audience from him. The only reason he had agreed to the meet was to check on the priestess' wellbeing. The message from Hermes hadn't mentioned exactly what was wrong, only that something was, which had made the gavel in Prometheus' gut drop like stone.

"There's no need to be a bad-tempered lion with me," Aphrodite admonished from her reclined position on a bench in the sun, droplets of water trickling from her still-wet hair onto the courtyard below in a steady *drip, drip, drip.*

"I have every reason, in case you had forgotten."

Aphrodite sat up and looked at him with rounded eyes that seemed to hold genuine sincerity. "And I am well overdue in my apology for that."

That was the thing about fickle Aphrodite, sometimes she had the ability to melt even the strongest defences. But Prometheus' motto prevailed.

"Actions have consequences. You knew what you were doing."

"I did not know how far it would stretch," Aphrodite countered in a melodic, measured tone.

It had been an eon ago since Prometheus, strong rugged Prometheus, had turned down Aphrodite's advances, long before the humans had been created. At the time, she had been so infuriated with him that when he'd asked for help making the human dolls seem less ... pathetic, she'd simply taken the opportunity he'd given her. She'd instructed him to place a kiss on each of their lips after Athena had given them the breath of life, so that they may experience the love and care their maker had in making them.

"I only omitted one tiny detail," she continued.

The kiss hadn't only given humans the love from their maker and unlocked all the emotions within them. It had also given the maker unconditional love for his creations.

"It was just supposed to be a harmless prank. I thought your foresight would have picked it up before anything came of it. It was petty of me. Can you see cause to forgive me?"

Prometheus stared hard at supposedly the most desirable woman in the world. Her harmless prank had multiplied and amplified as the humans reproduced. For every human mother that felt unconditional love for her child, Prometheus felt it too ... and now there were millions of them.

He shook his head. Aphrodite had been clever. She hadn't asked for forgiveness. She had appealed to the logic in him that he so often used as his moral compass. He could find cause. They both knew it. But, morals or not, when it came to his hatred for Aphrodite, he was not above lying.

"My heart is too hardened to consider forgiveness for you. No."

Aphrodite pursed her lips, her eyes narrowing.

"Very well. The least you can do is help me protect the priestess."

"That is why I agreed to meet," he replied with something not quite contempt but not quite sarcasm laced into his tone.

And so Aphrodite told him what she had learnt of Amara's time on Earth as she picked at the rose bush behind the bench she sat on, pricking her thumb against the thorns as she did so. Ichor ran down her thumb and curled around her wrist as she watched it. Prometheus watched her elegant movements too, her words causing his jaw to clench. The ichor, slower than a human's blood, stopped fairly quickly, giving the appearance of a silvery bangle wrapped around Aphrodite's delicate wrist.

"Funny how the humans associate blood with pain. Don't you think so?"

"Not really," Prometheus said, thinking of all the bloodshed over the years.

"Yet it is not the blood that causes the pain," Aphrodite reasoned.

Prometheus grunted, loath to agree with her internally once again but finding no fault in the logic.

"There are much more dangerous ways to cause a woman pain," she continued softly. "The fear they instilled in her was ... brutal. Unnecessarily so, in my opinion. And you know how I can be."

Prometheus nodded. He had experienced Aphrodite's vindictiveness first-hand, and that had only been meant to be a harmless prank according to her.

"She will break as a mere mortal woman if they keep up this tough-love plan Artemis and Athena have embarked on. She is not a hound to be broken in." Aphrodite's words continued to be so soft as to be barely audible, but her sing-song voice carried on the wind, making her words seem eerily premonitive and had Prometheus unknowingly nodding along.

"Perhaps, if she experienced pure love, she would alchemise the fear faster. What do you think, Prometheus?"

He contemplated his answer carefully, unnerved by the softness of Aphrodite's approach when his instincts screamed that she wanted something. "I am unsure why you have called on me to answer this question for you. You already know the answer. You gifted the humans their emotions."

Aphrodite pinned her gaze on him and suddenly she was the mercurial, demanding goddess he knew all too well. "Create her a mortal, one designed specifically for her."

Prometheus began shaking his head. "After what your sisters have already put her through? They will just use the mortal against her further. No. Teach her to love herself as you love yourself," he countered.

Aphrodite opened her mouth to reply but Prometheus stood, powerful thighs bulging as he did so. "No. That's my final answer if that's what you brought me here for. I will protect the priestess more heavily from now on, seeing as her own goddesses have forgotten the brutality of being human, but do not ask anything else of me, Aphrodite."

And with that, he turned his back on her, taking long, powerful strides as he left.

It was a rare occasion when Aphrodite was denied, an even rarer one when her pure intentions were dismissed. Prometheus had now denied both dual aspects of her and, for some reason, Pygmalion floated through Aphrodite's mind at that exact moment. Why the talented sculptor, insistent on not falling in love, would pop into her mind at that moment was odd. There must be a reason, she thought to herself as she watched Prometheus walk away, his tanned bronzed shoulders glinting in the last of the evening sunshine.

She had made the sculptor, intent on defying her, carve out his perfect woman in marble. Once he had done that, he willingly asked Aphrodite to gift him love so that he could bring his creation to life. All it had taken was using his craft in her favour. She had gifted Pygmalion the same technique that she had gifted Prometheus when he created the humans.

Still, her brain couldn't put the link together. What was it about the artists, beyond the method she had used, that linked them? Was it the fact that they were both stubborn? Something niggled at Aphrodite ... a thought that tickled in her mind, something that irked her, an itch she couldn't scratch. All she knew was that it had to do with Prometheus' almost callous rejection.

But, she realised, it wasn't the rejection of *her* that was sore. It was the rejection that he wouldn't do just about *anything* to help Amara. That was not the act of someone that should have had unconditional love for the priestess in human form.

Of course! Although the priestess was clothed in human skin, she wasn't a mortal soul. When she'd been gifted her emotional intellect, it must have attached to the soul not the skin of the human. Perhaps her memory had been reset, but the blueprint for emotional intelligence was already there. It didn't need to be crafted anew as it had with the rest of the humans. The curse had been circumnavigated. Prometheus didn't unconditionally love her. Which meant, Aphrodite realised with a start, that he could fall *in* love with her.

She just had to find a way to use his weakness, his taste for humanity, in her favour. And she knew exactly who to ask.

CHAPTER XI

"A game of dice my friend?"

Prometheus chuckled. "Against you? No."

The woman across from him managed to maintain a pout worthy of her mother for all of two seconds before it fell and the creases around her mouth turned into laughter lines. Prometheus grinned back at her, his large forearms crossed against his chest as he leaned against the countertop and watched her. Tyche truly was a beautiful woman. She was as voluptuous as her mother, Aphrodite, but athletic like her father, Hermes. Her cleavage peeked out from behind a modest dress, while her strong, lean arms were bare as she leaned towards Prometheus from her position.

"Go on, you know you want to."

It was a taunt between old friends, for it was a running joke who would prevail. Tyche, Goddess of Fair and Ill Fortune, or Prometheus' foresight. So far, in all the years they had known each other, Prometheus had only managed to win three hundred of the thousand or so games between them. Not that he was counting.

"Chess then," she countered, for she knew he could not resist a game of logic.

"Chess," he agreed before slowly making his way back to the table now that he had cleared the dishes of their supper away. Tyche went to the wall behind her that held cavern spaces for books and pulled out the old stone chess set. She knew where almost everything in this cabin was, having been one of the only ones Prometheus allowed to visit since he'd been sequestered to the confines of these walls in the mountain.

Night had descended, but there was a light that hung above the table that emitted a soft yellow beam so Tyche could see as she began to methodically polish and place the pieces in their rightful squares on the board, one by one, starting with the white first. Prometheus allowed himself a small smile. It was often an overlooked trait of Tyche's, her organisation. Most people often just associated her with chaos. Prometheus himself had been guilty of that in the past and was surprised when she'd revealed her Virgo nature. There was a messy imperfection to chaos, she had once told him. He had never forgotten it.

"Still as compulsive as ever," he jested, a rare joke from a man who rarely let anyone see this side of him.

"Look who's talking," she quipped back. "I hear you managed to get yourself entangled in the affairs of humans again."

"Who told you that?" Prometheus scowled.

"Aphrodite, of course."

"Is that why you're here? To do your mother's bidding?"

Tyche narrowed her hawk-like eyes, the same colour as her father's, at him and looked momentarily hurt.

"You think so little of our friendship?"

It had been Tyche that had appeared on his doorstep first, despite Zeus' decree that he was to be shunned for two thousand years while the God of Gods decided on Prometheus' punishment for presenting the humans with fire. Two thousand years was enough to set anyone's teeth on edge. Of course, as mistress of good fortune, she had known the time when it would be favourable to visit. And as mistress of ill fortune, she was used to being accused and blamed for things the humans could find no logic for. On paper, the two were unlikely friends. Tyche seemed impulsive and unpredictable, Prometheus logical and persevering, but they had found similarities in their rebellious, risk-taking natures ... and their absolute defiance to apologise for their stances. This, however, was not one of those occasions. Tyche was slowly teaching him the value of loyalty over logic.

"I ... apologise." The words came out like sandpaper in his throat.

"By Zeus, you really don't like to admit when you are wrong do you?" Then Tyche laughed, for she was not one to hold a grudge. Instead, she spun the chessboard around so that Prometheus faced the black. He scowled again but this time it held a playful edge.

"Really? You get to open?"

"Really? You think getting involved with the humans again is wise?" Tyche countered as she made her opening move.

"It's the right thing to do," he eventually answered. "Amara, the priestess, she ... deserves support in her task."

Tyche paused, momentarily stunned. In all the time they had known each other, she had always known her friend to be impartial unless his foresight was in play.

"What do you know?" she asked.

"Nothing, it's ... foggy," he growled, running a hand through the curls on his head in frustration before making a countermove. Tyche immediately responded in kind. A grunt was her only response as he kept his eyes on the board and she watched his facial expression in turn.

"Rusty from misuse, are we?"

"Something like that."

A comfortable silence broke out between the pair as they continued to play, making moves and countermoves until Prometheus was quietly confident he could win.

"Perhaps you are overdue a visit to the human realm," Tyche commented lightly as she moved her queen into check. Prometheus looked at her warily as he slowly moved his King into a more fortunate position.

"Tomorrow when the sun is at the highest point, you'll be able to leave unseen," she continued, moving a rook into a square that seemed to serve no purpose. "There's an exhibition in Edinburgh on the constellations I think you'd particularly enjoy."

"Why's that?" He grumbled.

"Because you should have been able to spot what I was doing six moves ago," she said as she moved her final piece into position and a checkmate was written between the pieces left on the board. "You are clearly troubled by this plight, and a troubled god – a Titan no less – is a dangerous one."

CHAPTER XII

By Wednesday the following week, Amara was retracing her footsteps once again, re-walking streets she'd already been down. Then she stumbled upon a conversation that gave her the unknowing answer as to why she was still doggedly here.

The tour guide looked to be in his forties or perhaps fifties; it was hard to tell with his silver hair and the side profile of his long, gaunt face. He wore an absurdly bright blue jacket and talked animatedly into a small lapel microphone, his hand holding up his collar. It was clear to see he was a spritely man, striding along chatting away to the two sets of couples following him, their hands crushed to their ears as they tried desperately to hear him over the roaring wind. Why would anyone go on a walking tour when winter had barely begun to thaw? Amara had no answer. Then again, here she was wandering the streets, so who was she to judge?

One couple, the larger pair, had stopped to take photos while the tour guide carried on walking in large strides. Amara caught a whiff of an American accent as the woman demanded her partner take more flattering shots of her against the backdrop of a large block of a building. The simplicity of the tan structure only further made its prominence and prestige more apparent. The simplicity of the woman, not so much. Wearing a bright pink leather jacket, leggings that looked like faded leopard print turned camouflage, and fur boots, the woman appeared to have stepped out of some Paris fashion show that had gone disastrously wrong in the high-street chain stores. Her partner was much more casual in jeans and a blue and white puffer jacket with a red stripe across the chest. Amara noted he wasn't being asked to pose in any of the photos.

She couldn't make much out of the other couple with the tour guide, their backs turned towards her. All she could see was a short, blonde woman with a tall, lean man clearly chatting to each other, obviously not all that interested in what the tour guide was saying. Amara was.

"Yes, that right over there is the National Library of Scotland. One of the largest research libraries in Europe! It houses every book published in the United Kingdom and keeps a copy of all printed materials too, from research papers to newspaper articles to birth announcements."

Birth announcements. It was a long shot. Amara had been left on a Parisian parish church doorstep, after all. But the visceral feeling in her gut lurched forward at the unexpected words and pulled at her until she found herself walking towards the building the tour guide had pointed out to his companions.

The inside was surprisingly modern given the exterior impression. Amara wasn't sure what she'd been expecting, perhaps more like the train station, but this seemed like any other reception hall she'd come across in the museums, libraries, and other such places in Paris.

Approaching the desk with no one ahead of her in the queue, she was greeted by a tall male with spectacles who looked awfully familiar, though she couldn't quite place him. His dark hair was long enough to flop just over his forehead and his green eyes were watery enough that they calmed her. His face was also rather gaunt, his body lost underneath the baggy grey jumper he wore, and the white shirt underneath left plenty of room for his neck to breathe. He felt … unintrusive. Perhaps that was why he was the first person she'd felt comfortable enough to talk to since *the incident*. Perhaps it was because he felt familiar and she couldn't quite place why, but she instinctively felt like he was not going to harm her.

"Can I help you?"

"Yes, I'd like to look for … ah … newspaper clippings and birth announcements from around twenty-five years ago?"

"Do you have one of our library cards?"

At Amara's dismayed look, he continued. "I'm assuming you're not from around here?"

"No," Amara said slowly, remembering what *he* had said about people of her complexion not being welcome.

The man paused before offering her a gentle smile that reached his eyes.

"The accent gave it away. Not to worry. I can issue you with a visitor's pass today. Unless you planned on returning?"

"No, I think I'll just have a look today. If that's ok?"

"Of course."

He drew his attention back to the computer in front of him, tapping away at the keys until Amara heard the whirr of a machine.

"Here you go." He handed her a piece of laminated plastic.

"Just head up the stairs and the reading room with the archives will be to your right."

"Thank you."

"Not a problem. You have a nice day now."

Amara nodded, careful not to smile at the kind man, and headed for the stairs.

After scouring the catalogues, she placed her online requests and waited patiently at the collections desk for them to appear. When the book fetcher – thankfully a woman this time – kindly handed them over, she carefully carried the copies of the papers to a nearby desk and settled in to read.

What felt like hours of fruitless searching later, Amara's eyes were sore, her head throbbing from information overload. Her body was stiff from sitting in the wooden chair where the cushion under the upholstered brown leather had been squashed over time, leaving little support underneath her. It had been a futile hope she finally acknowledged, placing the last newspaper archive back on the collection desk and heading back out the doors and down the stairs.

Whether it was because she'd been so focused on the archives when she came in or simply because she hadn't noticed before, when she walked back into the lobby, she saw signs for an exhibition. Checking the time on her phone, she saw it hadn't slipped by nearly as fast as she had expected through the myriad of newspaper archives, and she still had time to catch the exhibition. It was on one of her favourite topics, constellations. Following the signs for the building where the exhibition was being held, Amara was delighted to find it was a free exhibition to the public.

Stepping into the space, Amara felt her soul sigh. She hadn't realised her shoulders had been hunched up by her ears until they dropped down, the coil in her neck releasing at the same time. She took a deep breath of air and felt her ribcage expand. It felt like the first time she'd breathed in days.

The exhibition was wonderful. Projections on bare walls detailed all the different constellations, the written panes underneath them depicting their history. Not just their scientific discovery but the myths behind them all. Those were the stories Amara really loved.

She'd been lucky. Despite her penchant for exploring, she'd been given a lovely Parisian foster mother who had been strict but fair. Her one gift to Amara was that she had always told her a story about the stars at bedtime when asked for one. A moment of sadness tinted the exhibition as Amara remembered her. Remembered too the funeral, the feeling that she'd been abandoned once again and didn't quite belong now that her foster mother was gone. It had only been six short months after the funeral that she'd saved up enough money to leave Paris, after working day and night as a waitress, picking up any and all the extra shifts available.

Her hands skimmed along one of the display cabinets filled with old brown maps that were curling at the edges, depicting how the constellations were plotted, how they had developed over the ages, how one could still get their name on a star to this day.

That would be nice, Amara thought, *to be remembered in some way.*

As she continued to skim her fingers along the glass cabinets, peering at each piece on display, following the grooves of the panels that depicted all her favourite stories, she followed each twist and turn of the exhibition. Then, when she turned the fifth corner, blood roared through her ears as her heart pounded against her ribcage and gasping for air hurt. She wasn't alone after all.

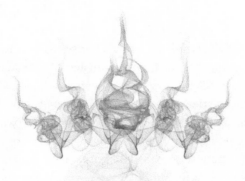

CHAPTER XIII

Prometheus felt the presence of another, like one feels the eyes on the back of their neck. It was an instinctive thing for humans and gods alike. The exhibition was closing shortly and he hadn't expected anyone else to be here. But there were two others with him, one a female that he could see out of the corner of his eye even now and another man whom he'd passed earlier.

Tyche, as ever, had been right and, as usual with her revelations, he could only admit it in hindsight, much the same way as the humans did when it came to her actions. He had been troubled and the sight of reconnecting with his siblings in the stars when he couldn't see them in person did something to soothe what remained of his soul. The melancholy of the past always helped him understand his gift when it felt more like a curse. He liked the Scottish lands too. There was something about them that reminded him of the earlier days when he had roamed amongst the humans freely, teaching them the arts they would need to survive and thrive. Edinburgh had taken those lessons to heart and it was a city that thrummed with activity because of it.

As Tyche had predicted, he'd been able to sneak past the Olympic barrier undetected by Zeus' eagle. Not that he thought the God of Gods could remember why he was mad at Prometheus anymore. He was probably off hunting heifers or his next conquest, provided his wife was kept busy. Zeus' selfish streak knew no limits. Prometheus almost regretted siding with him. Almost. It had been inevitable though, the Titans' future written in the stars. Here, in the stars, were the stories of their battles. Everything, every event, every loss, every win, every myth, could be traced back in the constellations.

Prometheus always felt the pull, the longing to understand his gift, his foresight, when it eluded him the most. And so, he tried to retrace footsteps to understand the past and make sense of the future. As always, it was fruitless. Like tying yourself to a shipwreck, hoping it would wash you out to sea again.

The feeling gnawed in his gut.

The goddesses had been callous in their plan for the priestess, and while he had told Aphrodite that he would offer the priestess more support ... that would only work if he could *find* her. While he knew she was in Edinburgh thanks to Aphrodite's insight, the city was home to over half a million humans. And it seemed as though she had gone to ground ever since her attack. Even if she hadn't, it wasn't as if he knew what she looked like. He had been foolish not to ask Aphrodite for more information before rebuffing her, and he didn't want to turn to Athena, for he knew they would only argue should they meet, anger still a dull ache in his bones at her actions. All he knew was that the priestess wouldn't look the same as when she'd met him at the cabin, given the human cloak he'd given her ... of that he was certain.

If Prometheus had still been in contact with the humans, he would have had a network of people to rely on, to be his eyes and ears to find her. But those souls had scattered to the wind and any remaining bloodlines were unlikely to believe the legends that their family line was once in favour with a Greek god.

While he understood the goddesses' plan to reintroduce alchemy to the world, he couldn't help but think of the last time they'd tried to bring magic back to the human realm. They'd burnt those women at the stake. Repeatedly. Each death had felt like a branding on Prometheus' flesh. While Amara would be using human tactics, he found himself still ... fearing for her. It was an acutely uncomfortable sensation. Worry for the humans he was used to, but this fear was acidic.

He knew what humans would do if they found out she was essentially teaching them witchcraft again. Now humans didn't burn what they didn't know; they ridiculed it. It was an insidious, black, crawling thing that covered them like slick hair gel, the fear. It spread until it silenced anyone they didn't understand with mocking laughter and dismissive tones. The mouths of laughter opened like caverns and unless you knew how to fight it, the fear that bubbled in those caverns would swallow you whole until there was a black vortex, an empty space, a void where your soul had been that denoted complete and utter annihilation. If they were to discover the priestess' true nature, they wouldn't burn her. They'd destroy her. Turn her into a shell of a woman, with no heart, no connection to her soul, no sense of purpose other than to serve the fear that drove them all. And because she was technically immortal, she would live out that reality for eternity, whatever form her body took.

Prometheus didn't understand why Athena and the others would place that burden on only one pair of shoulders. What did the Fates think was going to happen? That one priestess could change it all? What act of humanity could be saved by one woman?

"Excuse me?"

He turned his face and torso towards the voice, his arms still crossed against his chest, when he was hit by the sheer beauty of her. Cat-like green eyes watched him. They turned sharply inwards to a thin nose, with lush rosebud lips that rested underneath it. Her cheekbones were as sharp as her nose but softened by a speckling of freckles. Her hair was tied up into a messy bun, the few curls that had managed to escape were bouncing around her like drunken bumblebees. She was wearing a baggy green parka that swamped her, and black jeans that tailored her legs into brown boots with a small kitten heel.

She looked vaguely familiar, but then he'd known many humans. Sometimes he liked to play a game with himself to try and pinpoint the lineage between the human in front of him and the originals he'd created. A fun game if nothing else to puzzle himself over. He liked puzzles. But he couldn't quite place her.

"Yes?" he answered.

She pulled an embarrassed face, a light blush dusting her cheekbones.

"Would you mind pretending that we know each other?"

Prometheus' hackles rose.

"There's a man over there ... um ... and I think I may know him and I would really like to not be alone with him ... if it is him."

She was rambling now, unable to meet Prometheus' eyes. He reached out slowly and clasped a hand around her shoulder. She was so small that his hand covered the entirety of her rotator cuff. She flinched at the contact.

"It's ok," he said, his tone deep and slow and calming, for she looked like a rabbit caught in headlights. "But you need to pretend like you know me."

She gave a stiff nod and inched closer, though her body language continued to scream *stay the fuck away from me*. Prometheus' brow darkened at why she would have felt the need to approach a stranger she clearly wasn't comfortable with. Noted, too, the steel of her spine.

"Do you see this?" Prometheus took his hand from her shoulder and pointed to a collection of stars that looked like two boulders.

"Yes." Her eyes lit up, her breath hitched in her chest, but she was breathing slowly and she was listening to him.

"That's the Titan who holds up the Earth, Atlas."

Amara traced his fingers with her eyes, her eyelashes brushing lightly over her cheeks when she blinked.

"And there, where the 'Y' seems to shoot up into a star, that's Aquila, Zeus' eagle. He placed the image of his eagle in the sky to commemorate all his bird had done for him."

"You speak as if you know him."

"I suppose I do." Prometheus chuckled heavily, scratching at his three-day-old stubble. He glanced at Amara who was giving him a funny look.

"How do you know so much about the Greek gods?"

Prometheus shrugged. "Spent a lot of time studying them."

She continued to eye him warily.

"Why are you being so nice to me?"

Her cheeks flushed again, as if she was aware of how uncourteous it was to demand a stranger's time, their protection by association, and then further answers.

"Because you asked me to be," he said quietly.

She started to open her mouth, then shut it again.

"I'm ..." he went to tell her his name but realised she wouldn't believe him if he told her, so he settled for a varnished version of the truth.

"Theo, by the way. So you don't feel like you're talking to a stranger." At her wide-eyed look, he knew instinctively what she was panicking about. "You're under no obligation to give me yours."

She took a noticeable sigh and nodded back; her hands remained firmly tucked into the pockets of her parka. Prometheus most certainly wasn't getting a handshake.

Perhaps, if he had, he'd have realised that warmth radiating through him wasn't his usual protective love for his creations coming to the fore, but something much more tinged with Aphrodite's mark.

The sound of measured steps walking towards them, echoing and bouncing off the marble flooring had both Amara and Prometheus turning around. A tall, bird-like woman approached them. It wasn't simply the hook nose that gave the impression of a beak, but the high, white Victorian collar and the severity of her grey hair pulled back into a tight bun that illuminated her forehead and pointed chin, an unfortunate combination.

"I'm terribly sorry, dears, but this exhibition is now closed. I'm going to have to ask you both to make your way towards the exit."

The exit, which the woman in question had come from, was right behind them to their left. There was no sign of the other man, the one Amara had been too terrified to potentially bump into alone enough to approach a stranger. The bird woman continued to stand there, unmoving from her spot, practically ushering them out of the door with her stoicism. Once outside, they both stood under the robust stone brick entranceway. In good old traditional Scottish style, it had begun raining and the dark had seeped into the night sky. Time had flown after all. Amara worried at her lip with her teeth, taking a chunk of skin with it.

"Thank you ... for before," Amara clarified.

"I was happy to assist."

Prometheus gazed intently at Amara, but she only made eye contact for a split second before turning her own gaze away and biting back tears.

"I feel like I owe you something." She laughed.

"You don't owe me anything."

When she didn't say anything, Prometheus took her silence as his cue to leave.

"Would you like me to call you a taxi?"

She shook her head.

Prometheus mistook her shake as a sign to leave her alone.

"Well, it was nice to meet you. Take care," he said softly.

"Wait ..."

He turned back to face her and watched again as she lowered her head in embarrassment to hide her face. Whoever had done a number on this poor woman deserved to be pounded into the ground until they were dust, he thought.

"I, uh ... don't like taxis. But I also don't like walking alone in the dark. Would you ... would you mind if ..."

"I can walk with you," he said immediately and he noticed her shoulders visibly relax until her glance went beyond him. Turning, Prometheus saw a short man wearing a blue cap that had blonde hair flicking out underneath either side of it. His baseball jacket and baggy beige trousers didn't make him look particularly threatening. If anything, he looked like your average run-of-the-mill human. His companion had gone sheet white nonetheless.

"You want to get going?"

Her eyes darted back to Prometheus, the fear an insidious black thing that crawled behind her eyes. So, she was already acquainted with the worst of humanity's traits. A pity. A damn pity, Prometheus thought.

A sharp nod from Amara and Prometheus was striding out into the rain, Amara's hurried footsteps clipping shortly behind him until she caught up to his stride. She didn't tell him which way to go, but he figured he would wait until the other man was out of earshot and she relaxed once again. For now, she kept her arms firmly crossed against her chest as they walked against the wind, which was beginning to pick up. She walked along the edge of the street, flirting with the gutter.

It irked Prometheus. Usually, he'd have preferred to have her on his inside, closer to the safer side of the walkway. But she seemed more comfortable walking at the edge so when they turned the corner up ahead, she wouldn't bump into anyone, he supposed. He was getting the sense that this woman was big on personal space. The thought of what must have happened to ensure that protection was at the forefront of her mind made the colour of Prometheus' assumptions darken until she suddenly stopped.

"Everything ok?" He turned to her.

"I forgot. I need to grab something for dinner," she said nervously.

"I could eat."

She chanced another look at him, caught him grinning at her.

"I have no idea where around here is good," she said.

"I do. There's actually a really great place just up around the corner on the left here," Prometheus told her. He waited for her to nod in agreement, slowly because spooking her was not an option – she was far too intriguing – before leading the way.

A minute later he found himself unexpectedly laughing. Because for all her nervous disposition and manners, his companion couldn't hide her confoundedness at being brought to a chicken shop that clearly catered for the late-night drunks and university students. Luckily, it was still early in the evening so the shop was deserted apart from the young man behind the counter, texting on his phone.

"I swear, they do the best chicken in the whole of Edinburgh." Prometheus held his hands up, the size of small baseball mitts, still laughing.

"You better be right about that," Amara muttered as she bowed her head, brushed past him in the doorway, and went in.

It was the closest she'd come to initiating contact, and Prometheus felt a swoop of deep delight surprisingly roll through him. In truth, he had brought her here because he figured the casual setting would make her feel more at ease, though they really did do great fried chicken. He had seen enough fear in humans to know that home or small comforts could be like a weighted blanket against the feelings surging through their bodies.

The shop itself was narrow, two-thirds of it being taken up with the aluminium cooker tops and the counter itself, which separated the customers from the cooking. The

Perspex counter displayed a selection of cooked meats. There was fried chicken as well as battered sausages, an assortment of pizzas, and a separate salad and cold bar section closer to the cashier. On the other side of the cashier, there was a door to what was clearly the staff area and, Amara supposed, a toilet facility. Not that it was accessible to the customers, what with it being behind the counter.

She drummed her unvarnished and neatly clipped nails on the red countertop, looking at the menu up ahead behind the cashier and settled on a chicken box meal deal. Prometheus stood behind her and ordered himself two burgers, onion rings, fries, salad, and a large drink.

Amara's eyes widened at the order. Then again, he wasn't exactly a small man. Strange then, that she should feel so comfortable with a large male presence at her back. Then again, her abuser hadn't been big. Strength she had discovered, painful humiliating brute force, did not necessarily require a larger size.

Taking their seats at one of the four tables located opposite the counter, with its uncomfortable metal chairs and scratched-up fake wooden top, they waited for their food in silence. Theo appeared to like the silence. But Amara's mind was anything but a silent place. Thoughts raced behind her eyes as if she had a million things to do and a million places to be. Yet, here she was, having dinner with a stranger in a shitty little chicken shop.

"Miss, here's your meal."

The lanky kid behind the counter couldn't have been more than nineteen. He had a face covered in acne spreading from his temples all the way down to his chin that held a scrap of bumfluff. His ginger hair was tucked into a red cap that matched his oversized polo shirt of the same colour, which only served to make his skin look more inflamed. Amara couldn't tell if the lad was blushing at her or if he had the misfortune to have eczema too.

Theo kept his back to the wall as she returned to her seat, facing the counter rather than her so she didn't feel like she was being watched. But he kept an eye on her in his periphery and gave a small smile when he saw her eyes roll into the back of her head, her face infused with pleasure at the taste of her meal. Retaking his seat after collecting his own order, he tucked his legs under the table, his thighs brushing against the underside of the tabletop. There was a brief second where his knee touched hers.

Amara immediately jerked hers away.

"Sorry."

"It's fine," she muttered, her eyes firmly on her food.

"No, it's not."

Amara looked up to see him staring at her with those deep brown eyes intently.

"There's only one reason a woman actively avoids touch."

He could see her pulse pounding in her throat. He continued.

"It denotes abuse of some kind."

Amara remained silent. The lights above them flickered slightly. A couple entered the shop and placed their order at the counter. A chicken burger, chicken nuggets, and two portions of chips, extra salted.

"That man, in the exhibition with us ..."

"I don't want to talk about it."

He paused for a moment then tried a different tack.

"How long have you been in Edinburgh for?"

Amara played with the chip, swirling them around in a ketchup and mayonnaise painting. She'd lost her appetite.

Finally she said, "A few months."

Unwrapping the foil on his second burger, Theo didn't say anything for a while, his gaze lowered. It helped her not feel intruded upon. She closed the polystyrene lid on her meal while he continued taking large, measured bites of his burger.

Eventually she said, "I used to love meeting new people when I was back home. But now, travelling, nowhere feels safe."

Now she was talking, he tentatively leaned forward and braced his elbows on the table. Amara wasn't sure the weight of the chair he was in could actually hold the size of him.

She noticed his forearms, dusted with dark brown hair, bulging against the fabric of his blue shirt that was rolled up to the elbows, as if they were desperate to escape.

"What made you want to come here?"

Amara laughed. "You wouldn't believe me if I told you."

"You might be surprised."

She considered him for a moment and then, for reasons she didn't entirely understand herself, told him, "I felt the pull to come north. I couldn't explain it to you if I tried. I don't know if I can even explain it to myself."

"Like when the birds migrate." Theo nodded.

Amara gave him another assessing look.

"I never considered that."

"There's lots of things humans do that can't be explained, or justified." His tone turned dark. His brows furrowed over his deep-set eyes that were focused once again on her. But there was a kindness behind them, so even though her pulse thundered in her throat, Amara decided to be brave and share why she was really here.

"I don't like being alone."

He waited patiently for her to continue.

"But I suppose that's probably quite common for orphans." She smiled sadly. "That's why I was actually in the library today. I was looking at birth announcements. I thought maybe the urge to come here was somehow linked to discovering more about my heritage."

She glanced at Theo, who was still watching her with those eyes that said they'd seen more pain than she would ever know.

"Stupid, I know."

"No," he shrugged, tentatively leaning back in his chair. "I get it."

"Anyway, it was a complete waste of time. Nothing came of it. I should just go back to the parish and forget about it." She sighed, shaking her head as two more loose curls escaped her bun. The fluorescent light above them continued to flicker. Amara wasn't sure which of the two was more annoying.

It was a flippant comment she'd made, one they both knew she didn't mean. The fire that had bought her all the way here wasn't about to be snuffed out because she'd been subjected to abuse of some kind. No one determined enough to travel alone, on an instinct few would understand, was so flippant when turning their back on what could be considered a fated hand.

"Parish?" he asked.

"I was left as a baby on a parish church doorstep in Paris," she told him. "Father Michel practically raised me, even when I was in and out of foster homes. But I'd thought, seeing as I'd been wrapped in a tartan blanket that it must have been some clue ... some ... what?"

Theo was looking at her as if she'd just grown another head.

"What did you say?"

Prometheus didn't hear her response, his mind slow, stupid, unable to connect the dots until this moment. Until she'd literally spelled it out for him.

An unknown lineage. Paris. Parish church doorstep.

He'd found the priestess. Or, rather, she'd found him.

CHAPTER XIV

A thena watched a dot on a dusty-pink dawn horizon until it became bigger and bigger, stretching out like an ink dot on a page would. Soon, its form started to take shape and the tawny owl she had been expecting came into view, its wingspan magnificent. She watched its flight path, the sun glinting off its gold, bronzed, and occasional white feathers as it swept through the clouds until it landed, settled on her windowsill with a shake of its feathers and watched her with a patient expression, knowledge of what had happened in Edinburgh reflected in its eyes. Athena had learnt how to communicate with the birds through watching her father communicate with his eagle.

Wrapping Amara in that tartan had been no coincidence. Of course the child would think it was a clue to her lineage. Humans were so desperate to belong somewhere that they would go to any lengths to seek out their heritage. Perhaps, Athena thought, that is what the Moirai had meant when they had said the fear of abandonment would serve her.

Athena had needed Amara in Caledonia, the ancient name they had given to Scotland when the Greeks had begun to migrate there centuries ago. They just hadn't known *when* she would journey there or if she would indeed do it because she remembered the plan before she'd been incarnated on Earth. In Greek, Scot was *Skotia*, meaning the absence of light. It was the best place for the priestess to put her alchemy skills to the test and show humanity a new way of being. One led by faith rather than fear. One led by alchemy. One ... led by light.

The brutalisation had been a necessary evil, Athena continued to justify to herself. The mortal in question was no longer a problem. She'd dealt with him swiftly after he'd followed Amara to the library. A word with one of the wind goddesses and he'd simply "slipped" into traffic, bleary eyed with whisky on his breath. It was no real loss to humanity. Athena had no care why the mortal had done what he'd done, whether the man was emotionally damaged or not, like others – like Prometheus – perhaps might. All she cared about was that she had been made to look a fool. The human had laid his hands on *her* priestess and she could squash him like a bug for his actions. So she did. It helped with the smart of failure, a little.

If it would not interfere with her task, Athena would have cast Amara in the Gorgon Medusa's image. The serpents and cold-stone gaze had earned Medusa a reputation that ensured she'd never be taken advantage of again. Indeed, many human women had taken the lesson to heart, hardening themselves to further pain. It was necessary armour against the men who thought to take what was not theirs. But if she made Amara hideous to the humans, they wouldn't listen to her teachings. Fickle creatures that they were, they were still so concerned with the aesthetics that cast them in the gods' images, even though they no longer believed in those gods. So Amara had to remain beautiful, open, and vulnerable if they were to listen to her. Vulnerability was not something she often considered a useful tool. It set Athena's teeth on edge.

As did the thought that Aphrodite had outwitted her. She hadn't suspected her sister would manage to play Prometheus' protective instincts to her advantage. To get him to be the one to break through Amara's shell. It was an ingenious move.

Athena hadn't dared approach him, because she knew telling him of the Moirai's boon would have had him outraged that she had once again agreed to use humanity for her dirty work. He didn't understand the cost of battle. None of them did.

She wondered what Aphrodite had told him ... or offered him. However she had managed it, given her history with him and the fact he was one of the most defiant, stubborn gods Athena knew – especially when he'd been made a fool of – was quite a feat.

"Fair play, Aphrodite," Athena muttered under her breath. Because she hadn't been able to get anyone close to Amara. Despite Hera's 'no meddling' rule, it was usually easy enough for gods and goddesses to whisper things in the right human ears and get them to act 'of their own accord' when need be. But Amara had shunned anyone who had attempted to come near her. Anyone that was until Prometheus.

Athena stared at the still-empty, gnarled war table out of habit and debated her next move. She needed Amara to start her alchemy lessons, the trials of the seven 'sins'. Athena snorted at the thought.

Sending in the wrong god with the wrong lesson would only drive the priestess into a stupor. She needed one that was jarring, that would cause resistance in Amara's blood the minute it hit her. For resistance was the opposing force to acceptance. The sooner Amara accepted her gifts, the quicker they could get to work alchemising the fear. Given the way she had been exposed to it, Athena reasoned that the best lesson to send Amara first was lust.

Eros, God of Lust and Primal Desire, could easily be persuaded to prick her with an arrow. And if Prometheus remembered his vow, he would know to aid Amara through the challenge. If Amara could ride the waves of lust until she stopped fearing the intimate acts it would lead to, then she would be one step closer to remembering her alchemy.

Athena looked at her tawny companion who cooed in agreement. A cunning smile broke out over her face, pearl white canines glistening in the early spring morning sunshine. It looked like she'd be able to play Aphrodite's countermove to her advantage after all.

CHAPTER XV

They walked in silence down the cobbled street after dinner. Despite his earlier strange behaviour when she'd finally told him her name, which he'd brushed off as a strange sense of déjà vu, it was a comfortable silence that stretched between them.

Amara had forgotten how much she enjoyed the night. The way the streetlights twinkled and shimmered in the spring puddles on the pavement, the huge chasm of sky that was such a deep blue it almost appeared black. With Theo beside her, she felt safe for some reason. He kept his hands deep in his pockets and had made no move to touch her in any way. In fact, he actively made space when a lone passer-by tried to walk too close to her. She thought he was wonderful for it.

Eventually they reached the bottom of the stone steps that led to Amara's hotel.

"Thank you," she said softly. "I wasn't expecting today to be quite so, so …"

"... magical," he finished for her.

There was a look in his eyes she couldn't quite place. It was the same one he'd given her earlier, and it made her feel like she must have tomato sauce on her face. She wiped at her cheeks, just in case, but came away with clean hands.

"Would you like to do this again?" he asked her.

Amara let out a shy smile, unaware that it lit up her whole face.

"I would."

"Would tomorrow be too soon? I could show you some of my favourite areas of the city I think you'd love in the daylight," he offered.

"I'll be ready at eleven."

He nodded in agreement, rocking back on his heels, his hands still deep in his pockets.

"I'll see you tomorrow then."

"Yes. Goodnight."

"Goodnight."

She turned at the top of the entranceway stairs and saw him still waiting there until she was safe inside. When she made it to her room in the building, Amara turned the light on and went to the window to check if he was still there. He was. Then Theo lifted his hand in a wave and strolled into the night.

The next morning Theo was standing on the same spot, at 11 a.m. precisely, waiting for her. Dressed in jeans that moulded to his large legs and a deep V-neck black sweater with a matching black coat thrown over the top, he looked ... *gorgeous*. The thought startled Amara and she shook her head as if trying to shake it out. Look what had happened when she had let a stranger ogle her, and now she was doing the same thing!

"I am a fool," she muttered to herself as she headed down the stone steps towards him.

"Ready?" he asked. She nodded in return, not trusting herself to speak with her current thoughts, and together they began walking in what she assumed was the way to the city centre.

Their first stop was a bagel cart.

"We'll take two smoked salmon and cream cheese bagels and two coffees. Do you want milk or sugar in yours?"

Amara shook her head, pulling a face, and Theo grinned. Handing over the bagel, she contemplated admonishing him for ordering for her. But one bite in and the explosion of the freshness of the salmon coupled with the creaminess of the spread had her moaning out loud in delight. She blushed, embarrassed that she'd made such a loud sound. His eyes merely crinkled in delight at her, and they continued on their way. They walked past shops that looked like barbers, which he assured her were actually hidden underground pubs. They walked along rows of houses with private access to large gardens that looked beautiful even in early spring, when winter was still thawing. They walked through streets with quotes written on the pavement slabs if you knew where to look. Amara would have missed them completely if he hadn't pointed them out to her. She always had a habit of looking up at the sky when she walked, not down at her feet, as if she wanted to be in the heavens and not on Earth.

A week passed and Theo continued to show up for her. Every day, waiting on that same spot, precisely at 11 a.m. Every day a new hidden gem of the city revealed to her. Every day a little bit more comfortable in her own skin again.

Amara sighed, leaning back on the park bench they'd stopped at on the seventh day, on a walk around the gardens beneath the castle, staring up at the sky once again.

"Do you want to go up there?"

"Why don't we sit here a while?" The weather had proven favourable, though dark storm clouds loomed ominously across the way.

Together they sat, just enough space between them that Amara didn't feel intruded upon, and she found herself irked by it. As if she was now such damaged goods that she would forever be the broken butterfly to be protected rather than seen as a sensual woman again. *Where on earth were these thoughts coming from?* She was happy, she was safe, she was just grateful she no longer broke out in a cold sweat every time someone approached her, she reminded herself scoldingly.

"You know, they put plays on here in the summer," Theo told her, interrupting her thoughts. "Right there is where they usually do Shakespeare's *A Midsummer Night's Dream.*"

"Oh I loved that one!" Amara said with a laugh. "I played Titania in school but I always much preferred the character of Puck."

Theo threw his head back, the strong cords in his neck bulging as he let out a deep laugh. "That probably says a lot more about you than you want me to know."

Amara didn't even realise she was staring at his neck until she looked up and he appeared to be waiting patiently for her to reply to a question she hadn't heard.

"Sorry, what did you say?"

"I asked if you were hungry after all that walking. There's a little street vendor in the park that does a great pork and apple bun."

Amara scowled. "Do you only ever eat street food?" It had been all he'd offered her during their week of exploring together. She wasn't so damaged that she didn't notice he was feeding her comfort food. Again the knowledge irked at her.

"I mean you must eat proper meals. Look at you," she continued, gesturing to the bulk of him.

He smiled.

"A proper meal is what you want? A proper meal we shall have." He stood and this time he held out his hand to her. It was the first time Theo had offered physical contact since she'd flinched when he'd held her shoulder in the exhibition. Her heart thudded in her throat. It was a risky move on his part, but some instinct told her Theo never made risky moves unless he was almost certain they'd pay off.

She placed his hand in his.

The contact floored him. He felt the ichor run to his fingertips, the oath tugging into place firmly. The sheer strength of the bond was overwhelming. He felt instincts, old, *old* instincts rise to the fore. One by one, they roared to life, some he recognised, others he hadn't felt in eons. One was … new. Different. Odd. He rode the wave as each one ignited until he felt like he was burning up with it. Like the only way to get the heat off his back was to jump into the abyss, a cliff he hadn't realised he was standing over.

He kept his back straight, muscles bunched, trying to not freak Amara out with the sheer weight of it all. Instead, he grounded into the weight of her palm in his. Her soft, small palm. He stroked the back of her hand, focusing on the feeling of her warm skin, soothing him until the flame of emotion retreated into dancing embers that settled in his chest. It felt like a crater had blasted through his chest and now there was molten lava quietly pulsing where his heart should have been.

"Ready?" Amara asked, a quizzical look on her face.

"Yes."

Together they strolled to a café that looked busy but not full for a Wednesday lunchtime. That was always a good sign that the food would be excellent. He introduced Amara to haggis, and to his surprise, she tucked into it without so much as pulling a face. She wolfed down neeps and tatties before joining him in a whisky that burned the back of his throat and brought tears to both their eyes. He watched her carefully as she finished taking careful measured bites of the cute traditional Scottish cranachan that was held in the chocolate mould shaped like a cupcake, which had made her sigh when it arrived on the table. The way her tongue flicked over the final scoop of cream on her teaspoon before she sucked it clean made his trousers painfully tight.

"And I thought I could eat," he murmured.

"Well, I was hungry." Amara shrugged, defiantly. This bad-tempered version of her he liked. It was much better than the protective little mouse she'd been before. The fire in her called to him like a siren song.

Her stomach the next day, however, did not agree with the fact that she had gorged to the point of overindulgence. She hadn't vomited since she'd finally had the nerve to talk to another stranger again after *the incident*, though she still woke up in night sweats sometimes. On those nights, she always had to get up to triple check the doors and windows were locked, before turning a light back on to help her get back to sleep.

But this feeling gnawing at her stomach was far worse. It felt like being stabbed with sharp, hot pokers. Her bowels protested and her monthly bleed arrived at the same time. *Brilliant. Just fucking brilliant.* On little sleep, the dull fatigue made her body feel heavier than usual. Her arms and legs felt weak and jelly-like. So she took to lying on the cool grey bathroom tiles waiting for the next round of cramps.

There was a knock on her door. Tentatively, she made a move to sit up against the bathroom wall and another cramp ripped through her, shredding her insides. She groaned, moving back to her porcelain seat. Moving towards the door was not an option. The visitor knocked twice more, but Amara was too weak to even call out.

What seemed like hours passed before she managed to stand shakily and wash her face when there was another knock. She shuffled out of the bathroom slowly, manoeuvring between the tiny space of her bed and the mini wardrobe to her right, before she reached the door. Opening it she found a white plastic bag, tied at the top into a bow. On a Post-it note attached to the bag, written in a strongly slanted curve, it read,

Could hear you calling from the porcelain toilet when I came by earlier. Here's some soup – Theo.

The little gesture made her burst into tears.

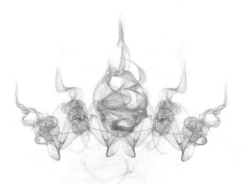

CHAPTER XVI

Prometheus had forgotten how wonderfully complex he had made them, the humans. Amara was such a walking contradiction in her human flesh. When he had met her in Olympus, she'd been polite, reserved, respectful, with a steel backbone underneath it all. All the things you would expect of a priestess. But now, that heart of wildfire only occasionally peeked out from behind a veneer of innocent vulnerability. She still possessed all the same qualities, but it was like they had melded together differently this time as they had grown with her human skin. And yet being around her was the most exhilarated he had felt around humans in eons.

When he had realised who Amara was, his first thought had been to tell her who he was, who *she* was. But every time he went to say it, the words sounded like the ramblings of a mad man. Instead, he'd decided to remain on Earth to support her. Zeus be damned. The challenges the goddesses had set would not be easy to complete and it was clear Amara would need all the help she could get.

If Prometheus was a betting man – and when his friend Tyche wasn't around, he was – he would have sworn that the goddesses had sent gluttonous Adephagia to visit Amara as one of the first of her challenges.

Adephagia was a robust goddess and that was putting it nicely. She consumed whatever was put in her path, her appetite never sated, her demeanour always one of dissatisfaction. If the goddesses had sent Adephagia to aid them, and she was the cause for Amara's indulgence at the bistro the other day, then the repercussions would be a purging. Amara would be called to purge everything in her life that did not serve her. The goddesses' plan would be for Amara to purge the fear. But from what Prometheus had seen, when Amara didn't know he was watching her, she still clung to the fear tightly, like a safety blanket made of pins that hurt her, even though she believed they protected her.

Amara had recovered from her gluttonous intake. Twelve days had passed since their dinner and they had met several times since. They were to meet tonight to celebrate the fact she had secured a job at the very bistro he'd taken her to. The spring air was getting warmer and warmer, and so he settled for walking to pick Amara up before taking her back to the pub that was underneath the rooms he always stayed in when he was in Edinburgh. Even though the evenings were getting lighter, and while her confidence grew with every day, he knew she still didn't like to walk alone.

She was waiting for him outside when he arrived though, which surprised him. He had expected her to wait, watching by the window until she saw him. Tonight, though, she opened her arms and offered him a hug. Her grip around his waist was fiercely tight, albeit brief, and Prometheus barely resisted the urge to crush her to him and keep her there. Reluctantly releasing her, his eyes scanned down her body.

She wasn't wearing baggy clothes tonight and, for the first time, he saw who she had been before her rape, which she'd finally confided in him the night after he'd sent her soup. A woman confident in her body, she wore black jeans that curved perfectly around her hips and a matching black denim jacket, a grey camisole underneath it. She'd paired the outfit with a tartan scarf and a brooch of a playful fox chasing its tail.

"I recognise that tartan," he murmured, reaching out and playing the fabric through his calloused fingers.

"You do?" Her eyes widened as she looked at him.

"Is it significant to you?"

Amara hesitated a moment before telling him. Her vulnerability broke his heart wide open.

"It was the scarf I was wrapped in as a baby."

"Ah," Prometheus said, realisation dawning, his eyes turning softly towards hers. "And that is why you ventured here."

Amara nodded.

He didn't know what made him say what he said next – that broken look of vulnerability on her face or the lava coursing through his veins when it came to her.

"I know where you can find more of this cloth. Perhaps they would have more knowledge of the lineage it holds?"

If she figured it out for herself, he reasoned, then she would not think him a mad man.

Amara stared at him in astoundment. "Are you serious?"

"Something I'm often accused of, but in this case yes." He chuckled in confirmation. "I'll take you next week?"

"I'd appreciate that," she said quietly. Then, she slipped her hand in his and they began walking.

"I like your fox," he said after a few moments of silence and pointed to the brooch.

"You don't think it's silly?" She sent him an uncertain look.

"No, sweetheart. I genuinely like it."

When Amara didn't say anything, and they just kept walking, Prometheus cursed himself. He had taken the change of clothing style as a sign that she was becoming more confident. But clearly his attempt at playfulness needed finesse. He wasn't a playful man by nature, he acknowledged. He liked logic, puzzles, solving things, fixing things. Confidence wasn't something he knew how to fix. Eventually he settled on what he knew she'd like.

"Have you heard the tale of Laelaps and the Teumessian fox?"

Amara shook her head. Her wild curls bounced around and Prometheus resisted the urge to curl them behind her ear.

"They're the constellations Canis Major and Minor."

Amara sent him a warm smile.

"Oh?"

"The Teumessian fox was destined never to be caught."

"Why?" It was less a question and more a demand from her lips, as if desperate that he reveal the heart of the story now. He loved the fiery impatience of her, even as he knew she secretly loved how the story unfolded more.

"Dionysus, God of Wine, sent it to the city of Thebes. They'd slighted him somehow, but it got blown up into an unpardonable crime."

He checked to see she was still listening. She sent him an impatient look in turn. He smiled.

"The regent of the city ... I forget his name ... well he asked for the use of one of Artemis' hounds, Laelaps, to capture the fox causing havoc in the farmers' fields."

Amara scrunched up her nose. "I should know that name."

"She's the hound destined to catch whatever prey she seeks."

"Who won?" Amara stopped dead, turned and faced him square on and folded her arms across her chest. He couldn't help it. He laughed and picked her up, swooping her around.

"You are a bad-tempered witch today."

"Only because you are deliberately dragging out the story," she replied, but she didn't tell him to let her go. Something deep within him growled in delight.

"Zeus didn't like the paradox it created. Two creatures designed to forever chase each other? It seemed to defeat the purpose. He turned them both to stone and set them in the stars."

"And you call *me* bad tempered."

Prometheus laughed again. He loved this side of her. And his arm was now casually around her shoulders and still she didn't shrug him off.

"Isn't that what humans do though?" Amara asked.

"In what sense?"

"Well, we're always chasing something forever, aren't we?" Her tone held a wistful note and Prometheus briefly thought of why she had come to Edinburgh in the first place. How she hadn't found the answers she sought. He wondered how much it ate at her. Unanswered puzzles drove him to distraction.

"Women who chase men, men who chase careers, those who chase freedom," she mused, warming to her theme.

"Crumbling struggles,

toils to be toyed,

grappling with grace.

Perhaps that is the curse of the human race.

Oh I blessed you with foresight,

But I burdened you with it too."

Amara stopped, looking at him with an inscrutable look in her eyes.

"Prometheus?" Amara hazarded a guess.

"Yes?" He momentarily forgot himself. Luckily, Amara took his tone as surprise.

"I have been listening you know," she nudged him with her shoulder playfully.

He shook his head clear. "Of course you have."

"What made you think of that poem?"

"I think that's why humans chase freedom," he answered quietly. "I think they know something better awaits them. It causes them to stop enjoying the moment and forces them into a perpetual loop of becoming better. It makes them the greatest creators of all time. And it steals the magic of their lives in the process."

Amara stopped once again and really looked at him then. Prometheus saw the pain in his own eyes reflected in her much younger ones. He went to tell her then, who he really was, why she was here, but then she stole his breath. Rising on tiptoe, she kissed his lips gently until he tentatively returned it. Then, burying his hands in her wild mane of hair, he kissed her back like a man drowning. It was a desperation that had both of them wanting more, until Amara's fingers curled into the grooves of his wool sweater and all he wanted was her hands on his skin. Eventually, Prometheus released her lips and allowed them to both catch their breath.

CHAPTER XVII

The pub Prometheus had planned on celebrating in with Amara was packed. He must have forgotten that it was a Saturday when the rugby was on, a true sport he could get behind. However, he couldn't stand the boisterous grown men who were childishly taunting each other as beer spilled over glasses, and angry voices were raised as the visiting team scored another try. The home team were getting their arses handed to them.

"I apologise for this." He noticed Amara's acute uncomfortableness as they moved through the bar. There wasn't much space between shoulders that continued to drunkenly try and barge into them. And there was only so much fending off he could do to protect Amara's small frame before they simply ran out of room.

"I'm staying in rooms above this place if you'd be more comfortable there?" he asked her, his lips practically pressed against the shell of her ear so she could hear him. Amara nodded in agreement with a smile that said she was eager to get out of the crowded pub and so they went upstairs.

The rooms, to Amara's shock, were huge. It appeared he had rented out the whole top floor. There was an informal living area upon entry, with a wardrobe just to the left, painted a ghastly mint green, with a little chalkboard sign hanging off the brass doorknob that had 'welcome' scrawled on it in a poor attempt at calligraphy. In the opposite corner, a mini bar was set up, just like the bar downstairs. Why there would be a bar when you could just go downstairs Amara had no idea. Moving through into the bedroom, she saw the carpet was a deep brown, the walls and bedsheets cream. Reaching out a hand, she touched the sheets to find them satin smooth. Opposite the bed was a wooden desk, above it a flat-screen TV. Then, as she moved around the room, she saw the door to the bathroom that had marble flooring and a deep free-standing bath.

"Well, it's better than where I stay."

"Make yourself at home."

Amara looked around but the only decent place to sit was the bed. Given how the dynamic had changed between them earlier, she felt uncomfortable sprawling out on it. She didn't want to come across as desperate, so she perched on the edge of it.

"Would you like a drink? There's a couple of mini bottles of champagne in here. We could toast to your new job?"

"Minibars are way too expensive. We can just go down a little later when it's calmed down."

"Price isn't an issue, Amara. But if you don't feel comfortable drinking ..."

"I've always felt comfortable enough around you to drink," she huffed. Perhaps it was because he didn't drink lager as Ralph had. Perhaps it was because he seemed content with just one drink. Perhaps it was because he carried himself differently. Amara couldn't pinpoint it. She just knew she didn't feel uncomfortable when she was with him in the same way she had with *him,* even before the alcohol had been a factor.

"I'm glad to hear it," Prometheus said gently, breaking Amara out of her reverie as he handed her a glass of champagne. They toasted to her new job and Prometheus took a seat on the opposite corner of the bed to her, one leg sprawled out, with his foot resting on the floor, the other hooked into a seated position.

"What do *you* do for a job?" Amara asked, realising in that moment how little she knew about his day-to-day life.

He paused for a moment. "I'm a craftsman by trade. Metal work, things like that. But I got out of the business a long time ago. Now I occasionally consult."

That explains his big, strong arms and where all the money comes from, Amara thought.

"How old are you?"

"Older than you."

Amara scowled and tried another tactic. "Any family? Are you from around here? Have you always been? You don't have an accent ..." Suddenly she was thirsty to know every facet of this fascinating man.

"Why the sudden Spanish inquisition?" he asked, though he had a crooked half smile as he asked her.

"Just ... curious," she shrugged. How was she supposed to tell him that she felt shy about practically jumping the bones of a man she knew nothing about? If she knew more about him, then it would make anything that did happen between them better than the last time she'd been in a similar position, she reasoned to herself. She risked a glance at him and was rewarded with blazing eye contact that scorched her to the soul, the electricity, the pull towards him almost magnetic. Amara blinked and glanced back down at her glass. She wondered if he'd felt it too. In an effort to settle the squirming uncomfortableness inside her, she took three large gulps of champagne until half the glass was empty.

"Never mind, it's none of my business. I shouldn't pry," she admonished herself.

"No, it's ok. It's just a long story, that's all."

"I like stories."

"I know." He paused for a moment, appearing to consider his options. "You may as well settle in then," he said, gesturing to the headboard. The pair of them stretched out on top of the covers before he began to regale her with tales from his home in Greece as if it wasn't the ancient civilization he'd always known it to be. She in turn told him all about the wild-child trips she'd had around the streets of Paris growing up.

As night fell, she asked him a question he'd never have predicted.

"Can I stay here the night?"

"Are you sure?" he asked gently. Amara nodded.

"I'll set up the pull-out."

Standing, he moved to the end of the bed. What had appeared to be a wooden chest for clothes actually had a camp bed stored in it.

"Oh you don't have to do that ..."

He paused and looked at her, staring into eyes of shattering green that stripped him to his soul.

"Amara," he said, a gentle warning in his tone.

Instead of backing down as he expected, she tipped her chin back in defiance. He noted the change immediately. The squaring of the shoulders. The locked jaw. The sharp gaze that was laced with desire and something ... more. If he focused for too long on her eyes or her full mouth, his jeans were going to become uncomfortably tight ... again.

"I'm going to run you a bath," he muttered. This was in no way a discussion he was prepared to have with her right now.

He filled the free-standing bath three-quarters of the way full and sprinkled an assortment of essential oils that made the bathroom smell of roses and honey. He also added a luxuriant bubble-bath mix, the light catching on the bubbles and making them sparkle from blue to pink between one second and the next.

"You know how to draw a bath," Amara remarked, leaning against the door jamb in the white linen robe she'd put on while he'd been busy. He could tell she was faking nonchalance but if it would get her to behave while his self-control was teetering, he'd take it.

"Hippocrates said that the key to health was an aromatic bath and a scented massage every day."

"Sounds like a man who knew his way into a woman's heart."

Prometheus chuckled. "And yet, he made those remarks for another man."

"Really?"

"Really." He tested the temperature with his elbow. "Come now. The water is perfect."

Walking over to him, she tested it with her hand, stood, and felt a shiver run through her body. Disrobing with her back to him – a quick hiccup of his heart – then and there, she sunk into the water until she was fully submerged. Only then did she look at him.

He was standing stock still, the muscles under his shirt he'd stripped down to strained, his jaw a harsh line. He was, very determinedly, looking Amara in the eyes.

"Yes?" she asked coyly.

"You should wait until a man leaves," he grounded out through clenched teeth.

A pregnant pause rested between them. But when Amara went to open her mouth, Prometheus stepped out of the bathroom.

When the bath water ran cold, and she'd perused and applied all the toiletries she could, Amara began to feel sheepish. *It had been a moment of insanity*, she told herself. That's how she'd justify it to him if he asked. Except it hadn't been that. It had been a need to prove to him that she wasn't just a broken butterfly, the maiden in distress he'd originally met. She wasn't the traumatised young woman he'd found in that exhibition. Ok, she was still healing but

... she'd been in shock then because she thought she'd seen Ralph again. Now, she knew it was just that – shock. She was perfectly capable of holding her own against a man ... against him. She had been for the past few weeks.

Wrapping the robe tightly around her, and leaving her hair damp around her shoulders, Amara tentatively opened the bathroom door. The cooler air, without the steam of the bathroom, slapped her in the face. It seemed to clear her head a little.

As she stepped out, she saw Theo spread out on the bed reading a book. His shirt had skewed slightly, revealing a thin sliver of bronzed abdomen and dark curls that had Amara's eyes wandering and mouth watering. A sensation she had always found acutely uncomfortable.

"Good bath?" He eyed her, sceptically she thought, from above the book.

"Yes, thank you." She shuffled over and plonked herself down on her side of the bed. The movement caused her robe to slip slightly, revealing a glimpse of smooth torso and bare breast.

He stared in turn.

She watched him watching her as she brought her hand up to where the robe slipped. When she let a small smile slip, as she chose to tease him some more by tantalizingly stroking at her skin ever so softly with her fingertips, he captured her wrist in his hand.

Amara froze.

Prometheus realised he had just done something disastrously wrong. Immediately he released his hold on her wrist but it was too late. The eyes that had been staring at him full and sensuous with desire a minute ago were now wild. Amara's muscles were rigid in a way that once again screamed *get the fuck away from me.* Her breathing was shallow – that damn robe was not helping him – and she watched him like prey watches a predator before it attacks.

"Amara, sweetheart, I need you to take deeper breasts, breaths. Dammit. Can you do that for me?"

No response from the woman across from him. He slid off the bed, making sure to keep his eyes on her as he walked backwards to the minibar to get her some fresh, cool water. When he returned, she had her eyes closed, the robe tugged firmly over her now as she crossed her arms, but she was breathing deeply.

"Here, drink this."

Eyes so pure and filled with so much hurt and pain, blinked open and stared at him. He got onto his knees at the side of the bed and gently reached out to stroke her hair. She didn't flinch. He understood immediately that it must have been something to do with her wrist. He looked down at said wrist to see her nervously wringing it. When his eyes met hers again, he saw the fear that flickered behind them. Still, she continued to breathe deeply and he continued to stroke her hair.

"You're not ready yet," he told her gently. It killed him to say it. He wanted nothing more than to wrap her in his arms and banish that insidious fear from her bones. He wanted to growl at any demons that came her way and keep her safe.

"You think I'm a child. You're babying me," she accused.

"No, I think you're traumatised," he reasoned.

"You think I'm broken."

"I didn't say that," he said, a dark anger beginning to simmer in his tone.

"You didn't have to." She pushed his hand away and sat up, swivelling round to the other side of the bed before stalking off to the bathroom door and slamming it shut. When she emerged, she was fully dressed.

His anger had continued to build as she'd been in the bathroom. She was so young, so naive. But it was more than that he admitted to himself, for he was a man who knew his own flaws well. He hated being shut out. He hated having words put in his mouth and he hated when his actions of help were thrown in his face. But when Amara exited, with her shoulders squared and a look of wounded pride on her face, the penny dropped.

Gluttony. Lust. *Pride*. He had seen the Goddess of Gluttony and her work first-hand on Amara. He had not, however, seen Eros strike with his arrow. That could have happened at any time, Prometheus reasoned to himself. The thought that Amara had only kissed him because she'd been touched by the God of Lust wounded him, but he couldn't think about that now. Because Hubris at some point, the third god to intervene with his own challenge, with his excessive pride, had infiltrated Amara's mind.

The goddesses, those two spiteful bitches Athena and Aphrodite, must have teamed up. They had been *using* him and his own actions against the priestess for her challenges. This was just a war move to them. Except it was clear Amara was losing every single battle to the fear. She had gorged without purging, given into lust but not overcome it, and now she was filled with a pride that would only make her defiant unless she could transmute it into humility. By the look on her face, that wasn't going to happen.

He was losing the priestess to her humanity.

All his anger redirected itself at once to the goddesses he'd be having words with once he was back in Olympus. The priestess was no longer – had never been – safe with him here on Earth, he realised.

He didn't know how Aphrodite had done it, but what he felt for Amara was not what he had felt for any other human before. He could admit that in the privacy of his own mind. And right now she'd be far safer away from him.

"I'll call you a taxi to take you home."

CHAPTER XVIII

Prometheus poured liquid metal into a casing and stood back, watching the molten substance hiss and spit as it settled.

He had returned to his cabin in the mountains after he had put Amara in the taxi and been here ever since. The journey from Earth to Olympus had only taken him a day once he was in the old lands of Greece. It had been a glorious start to the summer, with Demeter jubilant at her reunion with her daughter this year, but all Prometheus had seen these past three months was the dull grey of a life with Amara no longer in it.

Waiting for the mould to cool, he turned his attention to a black and gold gilded armour piece and began to stretch out his frustration on the fresh, tight leather.

"Prometheus, my friend."

Prometheus turned to see Tyche, swathed in a blue linen tunic and her hair tied in place with flowers, approaching him.

"What are you doing here?" Prometheus muttered gruffly as he turned back to the armour.

"The question is, what are you?" She gestured to the outside space around them where Prometheus did a lot of his work. Scattered around the courtyard was an array of cast-iron tools and unfinished projects, while sawdust from the woodwork Prometheus had done earlier swirled in the wind, scattering in the nearby garden beds. Anything to keep his mind off the small priestess who was roaming the plains of Caledonia.

"It would appear that foresight doesn't stop me from being foolish."

Tyche raised a manicured eyebrow. "Word from those who spend time in my mother's presence is that you are besotted with a certain priestess. I didn't realise it was this bad." Bad enough that Prometheus was back here effectively sulking.

Prometheus scowled. "I didn't take you for a gossip, Tyche."

Tyche pinned him with a glare, her arms folded across her chest and the comparison between her and Amara both scowling at him popped unbidden into his mind.

"I come with news of her, should you wish to hear it. But if you insist on being a bad-tempered oaf, I shall take my leave."

In her troubled hazelnut eyes was knowledge Prometheus wasn't sure he wished to know. He began to shake his head, his eyes cast back towards his work. But Tyche was not one for giving up so easily.

"You have not involved yourself in the affairs of humans for centuries. There must be a reason you did so for her," she said quietly. Prometheus turned to look at her and saw kindness he didn't want to see. It threatened to break him.

When Prometheus refused to reply, Tyche continued. "Hubris has made contact with Nemesis. He says your priestess has succumbed quite favourably to his prideful charms. He jests that she will lay in his bed forever. As you can imagine, Nemesis has grown increasingly more enraged." For those two had always held a sick contempt for one another that bordered on pathological possessiveness. Some mistook it for love.

"She has gathered Plutus, Aergia, and Phthonos to convoy with her to the human realm to seek retribution," Tyche continued.

Plutus, who was Tyche's son, though she had little to do with him, would try to convince Amara that copious amounts of wealth would strip her of fear. It was a trick he had convinced many mortals of. But Prometheus had told Amara of the fox that could never be caught. Surely she'd be able to see it in the greedy money game Plutus would play with her. *Wouldn't she?*

Aergia would send idleness, distracting Amara with numbing techniques that so easily surrounded the mortals. Indeed, Prometheus had designed the mortal form to succumb to numbness, when necessary, to protect itself. But Aergia had a habit of leaving her victims mindless, with no sense of passion or drive. He had seen the heart of Amara. She had too much passion and fire to fall prey to that, he thought. She wouldn't let fear send her there. *Would she?*

Phthonos would encase Amara in envy. Though how the spirit would do that, Prometheus had no clue. Perhaps play on her abandonment wound and her heritage, surrounding her with happy families. *A wound which he, Prometheus, had only made worse by leaving.*

He cursed himself for being so foolish. If Amara had already failed the gluttony, lust, and pride tasks the goddesses had set, would she really be able to tackle greed, idleness, and envy all at once? Especially led by Nemesis, retribution herself. A vein in Prometheus' neck twitched before he shook his head in defeat.

"I cannot aid her."

"There is more my friend ..."

Prometheus waited for the words. Though he was desperate not to hear them, he had to know.

"They have asked for Lyssa to accompany them."

Prometheus froze. He knew what the words meant but they wouldn't register. To send the goddess of mad rage, of frenzy, she who fed dogs rabies and turned them into wild wolves ...

"She'll kill her," he whispered.

For Lyssa's appetite knew no edge. She consumed souls until they did her bidding. Most mortals who caved to her persuasion ended up incarcerated, in one form or another. Or pumped full of so many drugs they were altered on a fundamental level. Amara would not be able to survive her onslaught. Prometheus knew of no mortal that had. Lyssa ruined lives and relished in it. A gentle soul such as Amara's would take out the rage on herself rather than harm another. She'd be more likely to take a knife to her own soft flesh and drive it through until she bled herself dry.

"I can see the logic as to why they are doing this," Tyche said gently.

Prometheus shot her a glare.

Tyche continued to stare at him kindly, and rather calmly for someone who was being threatened with a hammer. When Prometheus realised he was wielding the tool as a weapon, he regained what little composure he could and placed it back on the table with a small clearing of his throat. He made no move to apologise.

"They are hedging their bets and trusting that to herd her until her back is against the wall will leave her with no other option but to complete her task," the goddess stated.

Before Prometheus could berate her, Tyche spoke again, "You are a man who has built his morals around logic. The logic of their actions is valid, even in the same breath as it is flawed." Tyche took a coin out of her pocket tunic and played it through her fingertips, as if to further emphasise her point. "Surely even you can now see that logic cannot be held in equal measure to action where humanity is concerned."

Prometheus wrestled with the premise. Tyche had been a kind friend over the past two centuries and had taught him the value of friendship, of loyalty. But she had encouraged him back into that human world and look what had happened then, when action had not made space for logic. Amara had still failed even with his 'protection'. In this case, neither his logic nor actions, nor the goddesses', counted for anything.

The only one whose logic and action mattered right now was Amara. And she was better off without him.

"There is no argument, Tyche. They would use her against me. There is nothing more I can do."

Tyche frowned. To have her friend, who was usually defiant and unrepentant in what he believed in, say such things in such a tone ...

Her eyes widened as realisation dawned and a small smile graced her face.

"Aphrodite's spell does not work on an immortal in a human skin, does it?"

Prometheus truly looked at his friend then, pain shimmering behind eyes that had lived lifetimes.

"You are in love with her," she said softly.

Prometheus turned his back on Tyche, grabbed the hammer on the workbench and began bashing the shit out of an innocent plant pot that had been sitting there to be repaired. When, several minutes later, the pieces of it lay scattered, some on the bench, most having flown off in several different directions, Tyche placed a hand on his left shoulder.

"She is alone and in need of help. Your priestess does not deserve to be abandoned by one who loves her when she already believes herself alone in that world. Abandonment is a wound that is so easily ripped anew. Take it from one who knows."

"The humans only abandon you when they believe you have not found in their favour," Prometheus replied gruffly, still unable to look at her.

"You really think that Amara won't feel the same? That she has not been found favourable by you and that is why you left her? How do you think that logic will serve her when those other gods descend on her?"

When Prometheus didn't reply, Tyche continued. "Let me help you. I can assist but only where action is taken. Fortune, when she calls to me, favours the brave for a reason. And often it is in spite of that logic you hold so dear."

Prometheus felt the small hand leave his shoulder. Tyche, known to the others in their realm as impulsive and unpredictable, had never shared the method to her madness before. To do so was to reveal to another god exactly how their skillset worked, intellectual property that could be stolen. It was a huge act of trust, of vulnerability. It was not logical. It was a mark of ... loyalty.

His friend was right, he eventually acknowledged. Logic alone would not serve him when it came to Amara. It was true. He had equally failed the games the goddesses were playing, the perfect mirror to Amara's experience. He had retaliated to her defence mechanisms exactly as a human would. He hadn't realised how love – *true love* – would change his demeanour when in love with a human. How logic remained but was no longer the driving force. Aphrodite had been right and he had been wrong. Logic and love *could* coexist.

Now he knew he could do better, be better. Now he knew the stakes, he could outmanoeuvre each of those who would seek to harm Amara. He could protect her.

The only question was, would she let him?

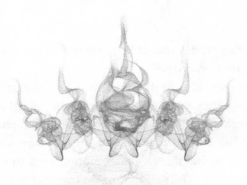

CHAPTER XIX

" Theo put you in a taxi, knowing how you feel about them, and left you," Amara muttered to herself, aggressively scrubbing the stainless-steel pot in her hands before before placing it in the industrial dishwasher. Whatever was burnt onto the bottom of it had refused to succumb to her fury. Of all the duties she had at the café, this was the one she liked least but it did make for excellent anger management therapy.

Amara hadn't seen Theo in three months.

She had spent that time throwing herself into her work just to keep busy. Her boss, Alice, was a broad, tall woman whose voice could boom across the café from the kitchen out back. But she was jovial and friendly and made Amara feel safe and protected under her wing. She also kept her busy. And while it had taken them a few weeks to find their rhythm together, Amara now knew, with military precision, how Alice liked to run her café. They worked in perfect unison, keeping the customers happy and coming back for more, day in, day out. It kept Amara's mind and body occupied from everything at least.

Until she was alone with the dishes. Then she was alone with her thoughts. What had happened when she'd arrived in Edinburgh. How Theo had looked at her that night she'd finally felt like herself again – as if she was a broken bird to be fixed. The fact that he had forgotten her fear of taxis and then left her. The fact that he'd promised to take her to that tartan shop and in the meantime she had gotten *nowhere* with it. It all played in the background of her mind in a perpetual loop. The fact that he hadn't come back at all cracked her heart open further and she let out a small sob.

"Are you muttering to yourself again?" Kiaria, one of the other waitresses, laughed as she came and dumped a load of dishes in the back.

Wicked smart and with a tongue to match, Amara wouldn't have expected Kiaria to be a waitress, much less Alice's niece. Where Alice was broad and fair in her late forties, Kiaria was a five-foot, petite Asian woman in her twenties.

"Adopted into the family," she'd told Amara the first time they'd met, at Amara's look of confusion she'd poorly hidden.

Kiaria's black hair was chopped in a stylish jagged fringe and finished neatly at her chin, which matched the cut of her cheekbones and jawline and made her seem incredibly no-nonsense. Like she'd cut straight to the point, and that was exactly what she did. Her eyes, laughing at Amara, were a deep, dark brown, so close to black that Amara couldn't actually tell where her irises began. But rather than giving off a cold, shark-like feel, the wide grin that accompanied Kiaria's heart-shaped face held a glint that was both personable and cheeky.

Amara smiled at Kiaria shyly, covering her sob as a sneeze. Then John, another waiter, who was a tall, lanky Northerner with sleazy charm coming out of his pores, entered. He snuck up on Kiaria and squeezed her stomach, making her squeal, and Amara turned back to the dishes.

She couldn't help the resentment that stirred in her gut. She felt cheap and dirty as she listened in to the lovers' whispered conversation. *Lustful.*

Then the guilt, for burning with such seething jealousy, would hit. They reminded her of Theo. Of what she was missing out on. *Envy.*

There was always the option, of course, to go out and choose a bedmate of her own. She'd had offers, which she'd almost agreed to a few times. But every time she got the courage to dress up to go out with the rest of the staff crew, she would take a hard look at herself in the mirror and remember that first night in Edinburgh, when she had been confident and secure in herself. *Look where that got you,* her mind would whisper. A shudder would roll through her body. She'd sigh, defeated, text Kiaria that she wasn't coming, get undressed, and reach for the bottle of wine that had now taken up a permanent residence on her bedside table in the shared house she was renting. *Idle.*

She was half convinced Kiaria had given up on getting her out of her mopey state. After her third offer was declined, Kiaria had simply resorted to raising an eyebrow at Amara the next day after she'd made a half-arsed excuse the night before. Usually the excuse was work. Days at the café started early, so it was valid and Amara certainly picked up the most shifts. She worked hard. She earned good money, she told herself. *Everything was fine.*

Yet when she would finish for the night, there was a collection of bottles her money was spent on, of all varieties, waiting for her at home. Wine, gin, whisky ... the collection continued to grow. *Greedily.*

At first, Amara had made the excuse that she was using them for something. A pretty blue and orange detailed gin bottle doubled as a vase, yet held a single red rose. Another had been used to store pennies. A third she was going to use for a sand bottle. She just hadn't gotten around to it yet.

If she was being honest with herself, she hadn't gotten around to much these days. Apart from work, she came home to eat, binge watch a series on the TV, drink, and go to bed. Upon waking up with a raging headache, she would punish herself by cleaning the dishes she had left from the night before, gagging at the smell of burnt meat. She vehemently chastised herself every time for forgetting to soak the dishes. *Furious.*

"Earth to Amara???" John interrupted.

"Sorry," Amara said, shaking her head and turning back to the pair of lovebirds, smiling sheepishly. "What did you say?"

"I asked if you wanted to come out with us again ... you still haven't been on a night out in Edinburgh you know."

Yes, Amara thought. *She had.*

"Ah no thanks, maybe another time."

John shrugged, clearly nonplussed, kissed Kiaria on the cheek and went back out front before Alice noticed and reprimanded him.

"What if we just had drinks, me and you?" Kiaria asked.

Amara paused her furious scrubbing.

"Just me and you?"

"Yeah."

Amara thought about it for a moment.

"Ok," she said, finding herself slowly nodding along. She could do that. After all, she felt safe in Kiaria's company. The fellow waitress preferred to do most of the talking, and while Amara could talk with the best of them, she much preferred to listen. Kiaria made her feel safe by taking the attention.

"Great! Do you want to do tomorrow night?"

"Sounds good to me."

The following night, Kiaria proved true to her word and managed to keep Amara occupied with copious amounts of wine and tales of her dating woes. Halfway through the conversation, she refilled their glasses with the remains of the second bottle despite Amara's protests. There was, at least, half a bottle in each glass.

Not long afterwards, John walked in and sidled up to their table. He was hard to miss. Aside from his height, his flaming red hair that crunched close to his skull and pale skin speckled with freckles, like Amara's own, illuminated him like a beacon. And given his height, his waist hit the tabletop as he snaked an arm around Kiaria.

"Fancy seeing you ladies here."

Immediately, regret seeped into Amara's bones. She should have known Kiaria wouldn't leave it. Some friend. In desperation to calm her nerves, Amara grabbed at her recently refilled glass and began to gulp greedily.

Given John's size, he was a man who simply took up room by breathing. Amara could feel his presence permeate her skin without him even touching her. It made goosebumps break out over her flesh. He sat, his legs brushing hers under the table and she immediately recoiled. Kiaria, in comparison, wrapped her limbs around him, entangling herself, like a fly willingly drawn into a spider's web. That spider was smiling coyly at Amara as she watched.

At some point, when the third bottle of wine was opened and sat on the table between them, Kiaria went up to go to the toilet. Silence hung heavy in the air and Amara took another swig from her wine glass.

"I get the impression you don't like me," John said, the smirk on his face saying more than his words.

Amara placed the wine glass back on the coaster, choosing her words carefully.

"It's not that I don't like you," she started.

"What is it then?"

"It's just that I don't like being around you and Kiaria much. You remind me of me and … it doesn't matter."

"So I remind you of your ex, do I?" John grinned as one long arm extended under the table towards Amara's leg, as if to clutch at her and lure her into him. She could practically see him preening.

"Kiaria will be back soon."

John shuffled his seat forward slightly and Amara felt their knees bump.

"You're just as beautiful as her, you know," he said, as his hand began to stroke her leg.

Amara froze. The last time a man had touched her without her permission had been before Theo. This was another stranger. No, it was John, she reminded herself. She knew John. Except she didn't really. Just like she hadn't known Ralph. Not really.

Her mind raced, desperately trying to convince her body that this was different, but it was no use. The fear coursing through her veins was like lactic acid, her limbs like lead. She couldn't move. She didn't dare breathe. It was like she was watching herself as John's hand inched up even closer. This wasn't what she wanted. She knew this wasn't what she wanted. Why couldn't she speak? Move? *Anything?!*

"What the HELL do you think you're doing?!"

John's hands recoiled like a snake so fast it was a wonder he didn't get whiplash.

Kiaria stood at the table, arms folded across her chest and a deep scowl painted across her face that turned the corners of her mouth down into a disdainful sneer.

"It's not what it looks like."

"I will deal with you later," Kiaria told him sharply before pointing towards the door. Hanging his head in demure agreement, John heeded instructions and excused himself. Kiaria stalked forward a step.

"And what the hell were you playing at?" she hissed.

Amara sat there, blinking, trying to get her brain to catch up with her body. She was so incredibly relieved and grateful that Kiaria had returned when she did, but her voice still wasn't working.

"You know, I could put up with the whole forlorn, woe-is-me, my-boyfriend-left-me act. But this? Going behind my back to try and make yourself feel better about the fact that he left you? It's pathetic. You're pathetic."

Finally Amara's brain began to function again, neurons snapping awake like fireworks crackling in her head. She went to open her mouth to explain, but Kiaria cut her off with a slicing hand action through the air.

"I don't want to hear it."

And with that, she stalked off.

Blood began to pool back into Amara's icy fingertips and toes, pins and needles flooding her extremities, the sensation akin to being on fire. She stood, shakily, and managed to walk to the local bus stop. Thankfully it wasn't too late and, thanks to the summer evening, it was still light outside.

The minute she was home she went to pour herself another drink and hesitated. Eventually, she thought better of it. Instead, she made short work of last night's dishes in burning hot water that scalded her skin pink. She scrubbed and scrubbed but the dishes still appeared dirty and she could not seem to get her hands clean, despite her efforts. Aggressively drying off her hands on a tea towel that rubbed her skin raw, Amara decided to hell with it. She poured herself a double helping of brandy, grabbed the blanket off her bed and decided to light a fire to enjoy the rest of the summer evening that was beginning to cool quite rapidly.

Inside, the anger was beginning to build. How dare Kiaria put all the blame on her?! Where was John's responsibility? Where was his admonishing? He was the one who had made the move and now Amara would pay the price at work. She wasn't safe here. She wasn't safe anywhere. She didn't even feel safe in her own skin. Amara still didn't quite understand what had happened, why she'd been unable to move, but that guilt just poured gasoline on top of a fire that had enough kindling already.

And this time, Theo wasn't here to save her.

Moving into the back garden of the house she had moved into in the three months since his disappearance, Amara set coals in the garden firepit with black iron tongs that creaked with age. She placed kindling strips and bunched up pieces of newspaper around them, as if arranging flowers in a crown. Finally, she topped the stack with the brick of a QuickFire starter and struck the match.

She got the odd sense that she had done this before. The ritual felt old, heavy in her bones, and the firepit reminded her of an altar. Her limbs moved slowly as if reacquainting themselves with old muscle memory, but the last time she had lit a fire had been in the chapel with Father Michel and it had been with a quick, mechanical thing with a long lighter that flicked with a switch. This felt different, ancient somehow.

The altar looked different too. For some reason, in her mind, she was picturing a water altar. One with a bath that was filled with spring waters and petals as the full moon passed over it, essential oils added with incantations as nymphs came to pay their respects. The fire couldn't have been any more different. And yet, somehow, the two rituals were linked. Amara just couldn't place her finger on why, and like those feelings of home that hounded her, those thoughts that teased and tormented her, the answer whispered just out of reach.

She stared desperately into the fire to get the answer to come back, but to no avail. *It must be the alcohol*, she told herself as she took another large swig of brandy. She enjoyed it burning down the back of her throat, penance for her inability to get the answers she so desperately kept seeking. Each question in her mind a cut on her skin.

As Amara sat there, listening to the fire crackle and watching the flames dance, the coals glow, and the embers spit, she became entranced. Pulling the tartan scarf, the one that she'd been wrapped in as a baby, over her lap, she began to hum. She didn't recognise the tune. Her throat opened and phonetic vowels fell out with a melody of a soft lullaby. The song pitched and fell effortlessly from her lips, like the coming and going of the tide, and the flames flickered in unison. She could feel the humming vibrating through her bones, the melody cutting through her lungs, the rhythm tugging at her womb, as if her body thrummed with humanity.

The water in her mind, the fire in front of her, the earth beneath her sit bones, the air in her lungs … it all added up to humanity. *That was the answer*, she whispered to herself as her eyes drooped, her head slumped and she fell asleep in front of the roaring fire.

Amara tossed and turned. The dream she was having morphed, and her eyes flickered beneath her eyelids. In the dream, she imagined someone was watching over her, a man with delicate features. Blonde hair that flopped over his forehead in a boyish manner. The eyes that were staring at her were a deep blue, and he had a sad smile on his face as if watching her sleep was bittersweet.

But then the man morphed into Theo and he climbed into bed with her. She could feel his arms wrap around her and she snuggled deeper into the curve of his legs. She could feel the coarse hairs of his legs cause delicious friction against her smooth ones and his hot breath tickle the back of her neck. Smiling, she angled her head deeper into the pillow to allow him better access and felt a rough kiss scraped with stubble against her cheek as his calloused hands began to move across her skin.

Amara awoke with a start.

There was no Theo in bed with her. She didn't even remember putting out the fire or getting into bed. Instead, the cotton white sheets were tangled around her limbs like vines. The window, which she usually made sure was shut before her head hit the pillow, was ajar and a cool night breeze blew out across the room, raising goosebumps all over her skin. Rising, wearing just a navy blue camisole and a pair of grey cotton briefs, she crossed the room and shut the door, shivering as she did so. She dived back under the covers and wrapped herself in the duvet like a cocoon. Burying herself deeper into the bed, she tried desperately to fall back into that dream with Theo, but it was no use. The fresh air had slapped her wide awake.

She looked at her alarm clock – 4 a.m. The sky outside her small window, opposite the bed, was a dusty pink that promised summer thunderstorms. Amara huddled under the covers for as long as possible. It would only be an hour until she had to get up for work anyway. That thought, and the fact she had to see Kiaria today, made the contents of her stomach curdle. She raced to the bathroom before depositing what remained of the alcohol in her stomach into the toilet bowl. She spent the next hour shaking and retching on the bathroom tiles before showering and trying to make herself halfway presentable.

By 5.30, she was out the door, walking down stone pavements lit by the early morning sunshine, a rare occurrence in Edinburgh she had learnt. Yet even with a thin red coat and the sunshine on her skin, she felt a biting cold that sent her numb inside. The only thing that would help was if she made herself a pot of hot black coffee to warm her up as soon as she entered the café. Then she could begin prepping for the day.

"Morning Amara, coffee?" Alice called out as she heard the bell above the door tinkle. She had caught on quickly to Amara's little routines. It turned out she found them quite charming. Though the coffee she offered was often as strong as whisky.

"Morning, love." Graham, Alice's husband, sent Amara a short little wave from the kitchen doorway out back. He was responsible for preparing the baked goods for the day and was carrying a load of croissants, fresh bread that Amara would now butter in preparation for the hot sandwiches at lunch, doughnuts, and an array of muffins. He set them on the steel kitchen table out the back.

Graham was a couple of inches taller than Alice, his hair and beard speckled in salt-and-pepper shades. He didn't ever say much more than a greeting. But when he smiled as he waved hello, his eyes crinkled at the corners. He had kind eyes. Between the two of them Amara felt safe, even as the thought of confronting Kiaria today ripped her anxiety wound open anew.

"It'll be a busy day," Alice told her.

"Oh?"

"Yeah ... Kiaria's just called in sick and I have no one else who can cover. I hope you slept well."

Amara forced a bright smile, her anxiety fluttering to a stop. "Of course!"

She got to work immediately slicing and buttering the loaves of bread.

Once the immediate food was prepared for the day, Amara set up the coffee machine, checked the tables, and then began on the back-of-house tasks, like sifting kilograms of flour into old, large paint containers for Graham's baking tomorrow and other assorted jobs. The tasks, for the most part, kept her busy enough that she didn't have time to pause and think.

But every so often, her mind would wander back to the dream this morning, which released a cascade of unanswered questions. Where had Theo gone? Why hadn't he said goodbye? What was wrong with her that everyone hurt her? Abandoned her? Left her? Blamed her? Would Kiaria seek retribution? What had John said? Would she lose her job over this?

Then the bell chimed as the first customer entered and the morning rush began. Amara's mind remained occupied for the rest of the day, dealing with customers, orders, and coffees. After the early morning commuters in their suits, surgically attached to their phones demanding "the strongest coffee you have" left, the mums with their prams arrived.

"Busy day, Amara?" one mum asked, as she pushed a pram at the counter and balanced a screaming two-year-old on yoga pants that did their best to hide the bulges. The child's screams continued to pierce Amara's eardrums until the dull ache at the back of her head turned into a full-blown headache. She tried not to wince.

"You know what it's like here!" Amara laughed it off, scribbling down the woman's order and handing her a table number. Seeing that a table had left, Amara went to clear it down, wipe, and reset. It held new occupants not even a minute after she was done.

After the morning rush, those local to the area would often stop by for lunch, though there were usually a few new faces every time given the reputation the café was building. But the afternoons were Amara's favourite, for that was when the old Scottish women would come to see her.

"Tell us, Amara, have you eaten today? Look at you … you're skin and bone," the taller and stricter of the two – Rhonda – scolded in lieu of a greeting. She took off her coat and draped it over the table in the window that the two ladies always took, despite the fact the sun was shining outside said window.

The table easily had the best seats in the house. Two faded red armchairs looked out onto the street. It was perfect for people watching, and the alcove provided by the window kept it far enough away from the other tables that you could have a good gossip as you did so.

"Leave her be. Can't you see the girl is busy?" Bessie, Amara's favourite, swiped at her friend as she settled into her chair. Her little dog, Bertie, a black-haired Scottish terrier, was the spitting image of his owner. Amara bent down to give Bessie a kiss on either cheek and then bent further still to give Bertie a rub on his tummy.

"I like your skirt today, Bessie. Where did you get that tartan from?" Amara asked, eyeing up the pattern that looked so similar to the one that had been haunting Amara all her life.

"Oh this old thing? I've had this for years! Why? Would you like me to make you one? I can, you know!"

"Oh no. It's just that I have a scarf just like it," Amara said, gently touching Bessie's arm. "I was actually looking for a tartan shop that could explain the lineage of it to me. But I haven't been able to find a store that sells the particular pattern I have."

"Oh well why don't you bring it to us next time we're in and we can see if we know it. We've been here long enough – we're practically historians!" Bessie joked.

Amara stared at her, wide eyed and hopeful once again. "I have it out back. I'll go and grab it after I place your order. The usual for you three?"

"Please. Then, after we've determined where your tartan is from, you can tell us why we still haven't seen anyone come and snap you up from this place. It's been months!" Rhonda said.

Rhonda was a firm believer, as she had told Amara many times before, that while there were times a woman should work in her life, it was to be a 'shelf-life experience'. And Amara was fast approaching the end of that shelf.

"You don't have to marry them for love, dear. Take it from me, marry for money the first time. Marry for love the second. It makes it all much easier. You can't keep working here forever. You'll get calloused hands. Women should be cherished not calloused in their lifetime."

Rhonda's own hands were adorned with two sets of diamond engagement rings on her divorced finger and one remaining set on her ring finger, though she was now widowed. Her late husband had been the only one she'd truly loved, she'd happily told Amara who took the advice with good humour and went about setting their teas and sweet treats and a bowl of water for Bertie. When she returned to the table with her scarf, Bessie and Rhonda eyed the pattern.

"Hmm, no I don't think I've seen this pattern before." Bessie said. "Have you?"

"No," Rhonda replied. "Where did you say you got it from again, dear?"

"I was wrapped in it as a baby," Amara said, a lump in her throat and hope beginning to free fall in her stomach.

"Hmm, we'll have to ask the others in our Bible study group. Here, you hold onto it for now, love." Bessie patted her arm.

At Amara's crestfallen look, the kind old woman spoke again.

"We are worried about you, dear. You do seem to always be here."

"Well, so are you." Amara jested kindly, trying to brush off the disappointment that had crashed into her.

"Yes, but we've lived our lives. What life is this for a young woman? We didn't burn our bras in the seventies, you know, for you to continue living a life of service to others," Bessie admonished gently.

"I'm happy here," Amara reassured her. And despite the turmoil and drama, it was true. Amara *was* happy there. Sure, answers still whispered out of reach and she missed Theo so badly it hurt, but she was otherwise content. *Wasn't that good enough?*

At the end of the long day, as Alice was out the back, loading the carrier trays into Graham's car for the fresh-baked goods and Amara was mopping the floor behind the counter, the door chimed open.

"Sorry we're—"

Amara's tongue went numb as she looked up. Her heart thudded wildly, threatening to take her to the floor with it. She held onto the mop like her life depended on it right then, her grip on the wooden handle tightening until the veins on the back of her hands popped, like dark blue rivers about to burst through the dams of her knuckles. Leaning on the mop was the only thing that grounded her, that stopped her from collapsing in relief or running to him in gratitude. No, that she would not do.

Because there, in the doorway, stood Theo, with knowledge behind his eyes that said he knew he'd hurt her.

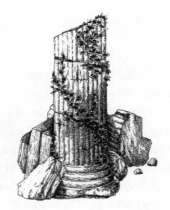

CHAPTER XX

A thena was not used to failure. But every single one of the gods and goddesses had returned from the human realm with callously cruel grins on their faces and patted each other on the back for jobs well done, unaware of the true nature of their mission. She had smiled in appeasement at them – for her instruction to them had been to cause havoc in Amara's life in the hopes the priestess would alchemise each challenge – while inwardly seething.

Aphrodite, it appeared, had been right. Willing to put her pride aside for now if it would ensure her victory – and the survival of the humans – Athena decided it was time to end this little feud. Which was why she was currently on her way to her sister's gardens on the northern side of Mount Olympus.

Eventually reaching the cream-coloured pillars that were topped with swans carved in marble and laced with myrtle flowers, and which announced the beginning of Aphrodite's land, Athena stepped into Aphrodite's territory. Immediately she was greeted by Dike, who, as the spirit of justice, often gave measured advice in Athena's counsel too. Why she chose to spend so much time with Aphrodite made Athena shake her head in despair. Dike would never understand that she would always be a justification, a reason, an excuse for both herself and Aphrodite as well as the humans. She would never hold her own. Justice by itself was never cause enough for the humans to act. There was always something she had to be paired with. Most often Dike chose to align herself with Aphrodite and so justice was almost always sought for the love of something.

"Lady Athena." She bowed demurely. "Have you come for Lady Aphrodite?"

It wasn't a foolish question for Aphrodite was often in the company of many.

"Yes."

"Please, follow me."

Together they walked along delicately winding pebbled paths, either side encased by soft, moss-green grass that was littered with red and white anemone flowers. As they got closer to the entrance to Aphrodite's rooms, rose bushes sprouted strong and proud from the soil, some of their flowers red, others white. All thriving. Aphrodite had always had a natural aptitude for vegetation.

At the large, stone-white doors with gilded gold trim, Dike knocked twice before they entered upon approval. Where Athena's war rooms were sparse, Aphrodite's rooms were filled with plushness. Red velvet chaises were artfully placed, with white column pillars beside them housing all manner of items: an intricately decorated vase detailing Aphrodite's rise to fame and life itself, a bowl of grapes, a pure gold decanter.

The floor covering consisted of one large silk woven rug, made by Arachne if Athena wasn't mistaken, the most talented spinner before she had challenged Athena to a duel. The poor girl had hung herself to avoid Athena's fury, and so she had mercifully turned the girl into a spider – for such talent was too good to be gone from the world.

Like Athena's war rooms, the windows were large enough that they gave a spectacular view of the gardens Athena had just come from, meaning her sister had watched her walk here. And waited. She was, however, not alone.

Opposite her, on a different chaise, was Dionysus. A goblet was raised to his mouth as he watched Athena assess him. If he was waiting for shock to grace her face, her youngest half brother would be waiting a while. He raised the goblet in a half-hearted greeting.

Aphrodite, meanwhile, sat waiting for Athena to make formal introductions before she rose from her lounging position.

So, Athena reasoned, *she is still furious*.

"Sister," she greeted her in a calm tone.

Aphrodite did indeed then rise and cross the space to place a cold kiss on either cheek.

"Athena, please sit. Dike – you may leave us now."

The door closed quietly. For several minutes, there was no sound beyond that of the birds frolicking in the garden. Eventually, having measured her words, Athena spoke.

"If I were to hazard a guess, I would say it is no coincidence that I find you and Dionysus in each other's company."

The last time they had been seen together, there had been rumours he had fathered Priapus with Aphrodite, a claim neither of them would confirm nor deny. Athena wondered if he was just here out of coincidence or if Aphrodite had roped him in for some plot twist to her plan as she had Prometheus.

"It appears you may have been right in your estimations of Artemis' plan."

"Oh?" Aphrodite cocked one perfectly manicured blonde eyebrow, but there was no surprise there, only vain delight.

Athena pursed her lips, her jaw aching under the pressure of clenched teeth. She despised losing.

"The fear took too great a hold. The ways – *our* ways – did not penetrate the priestess' psyche. She has lost her alchemy somewhere in the recesses of her mind. I would say true love remains a last resort ... but I know your hand has been long involved, has it not?"

Aphrodite giggled before plucking a plump grape and biting down on it delicately. She could make even that look seductive.

"Oh come now, were you not impressed?"

"How *did* you manage to get Prometheus involved?" Athena scowled.

Aphrodite crossed to another table to retrieve two goblets and poured them both wine from the decanter to celebrate, now that cold formalities had been acknowledged. Usually the nymphs would assist in such matters, but nymphs had a terrible knack for gossip, more so than anyone else of

Mount Olympus.

"Not intentionally," Aphrodite scoffed, handing over a goblet and resuming her seat. "The fool would not hear me out. Luckily for me, the Moirai saw fit to find me favour, and Tyche helped too."

"Tyche?" Dionysus interrupted, a small furrow in that round baby face of his that made him look, still, like a petulant child despite his many years.

"My daughter and Prometheus have long since been friends. Did you not know?"

"I didn't suspect the fickle goddess to be quite so friendly with one as stubborn as Prometheus," Dionysus quipped back.

"Careful," Aphrodite tempered with a sharp glare. "That is my daughter."

Dionysus raised his goblet in mock salute, though Athena was sure Aphrodite missed the sarcastic smile behind it. "Of course, I am here to help you."

"Where did the Moirai find in your favour?" she interrupted, for she was far more interested in their play than Dionysus'.

Aphrodite simply leaned back, raising her hands to the heavens as if she was presenting herself as the gift. Athena put two and two together.

"You managed to circuit break your little parlour trick."

"Thankfully, or we would be in a mess now would we not?"

Athena took a sip of wine, humming in agreement. While she could be a sore loser, in this instance she was grateful.

There was hope yet. "I thank the Fates that they allowed you to play a part I ... had not given enough consideration."

Aphrodite tilted her head slightly, taking the acknowledgement gracefully. After a moment's pause, Athena came to ask the question she was actually here for.

"Are you certain it will work?"

Aphrodite smiled coyly.

"You are not to worry that heavy head of yours with more burdens," she nodded, pointing at Athena's helmet made of gold that curved at a point on her forehead and gave the resemblance of a beak, a homage to Zeus' eagle. "You are not the only one the Moirai consults with. It is all taken care of. Welcome back, sister, to the winning team."

CHAPTER XXI

S eeing her standing in the doorway, safe and somewhat annoyed, if the little furrow between her eyebrows was anything to go by, Prometheus felt the punch to his solar plexus knock the wind right out of him. He had *missed* her.

He had always known Aphrodite was cruel, but he had no idea she could be so ruthless when it came to getting what she wanted. And what the goddesses wanted, as Prometheus had well and truly learnt these past few months, was to get their way ... no matter the cost to those involved. No matter who it hurt.

"What are you doing here?" Amara demanded, setting the mop against the wall and stalking out from behind the counter.

"You're dripping wet," she muttered.

He suddenly noticed he had dripped water droplets all over the freshly mopped floor. The heavens had opened just before he arrived, a bout of summer showers soaking him.

Amara pulled out a chair and insisted he sit, before taking a seat opposite him. She can't help it, he thought, hostessing was in her nature. The table, the one closest to the door and smack bang in the middle of the café floor, seemed to be her version of a firm barrier between them. Prometheus realised she wasn't just annoyed; she was angry.

"I'm sorry I haven't been around since we last saw each other," he began.

"It's fine. It's not like I needed babysitting," Amara bit back immediately, followed by a roll of her eyes and a muttered string of French under her breath, where she implied he liked to rescue damsels in distress or those with daddy issues, for which he was a bastard.

She didn't know he spoke the language fluently.

Rain continued to lightly trickle against the windows in a tapping pattern that was both soothing and irritating in equal measure. Demeter was sobbing. Her daughter was due to leave for the underworld soon, and she had begun her grieving period on the Earth early it would seem. Autumn was still a while away yet. But that was no matter to Prometheus at present. He was far more concerned with the anger of the woman sitting opposite him.

Amara wouldn't look him in the eyes, her body turned towards the door in such a way that suggested he leave immediately. It also only gave him a side profile of her face. But she'd told him to sit down, and he saw the tear brimming at the edge before she managed to blink it back.

So she wasn't angry. She was hurt. She needed reassurance.

He couldn't blame her. Knowing her history, her longing to belong, the abandonment wound she held, he wished he had some explanation that wasn't the ludicrousness of the fact that he had handled the situation wrong. That he hadn't known what to do because he hadn't told anyone he had fallen in love with them in ... centuries. Not since his wife, Hesione, and, well, that hadn't worked out. Clearly.

"There is something rather distasteful, I find, about the men who prey on the women craving their father's love. Says rather a lot about his character, I'm afraid," Prometheus said.

He got a look of pure loathing for his efforts at a joke. Humour really was not his forte.

"Amara," he tried again, gently but firmly.

"So you can speak French? What else don't I know about you?" The words were clipped, the tone sharp. The words of a defensive woman, a woman who had been vulnerable and then not been given safety in exchange. The eyes, ah the eyes, gave her away. They were agonisingly scared of the answer he might give.

He tried something he would never have imagined himself daring to.

Reaching across the table, he took her hand in his and then gently began to stroke the inside of her wrist with his calloused thumb. Her dainty hand felt tiny cupped in his big, bronzed one, her flesh soft. He imagined she must keep hand cream by her bedside, rub it in every night. The images that followed sent an inappropriate jolt through him and back into the present moment.

She sucked in a breath, but she didn't break the contact as he'd expected her to.

"I had no intention of abandoning you." He put it bluntly. It was the only way he knew how.

Her lip quivered, and she brushed a tendril of hair behind her ear, using her hand to keep her face hidden from him. Still she didn't say anything. When she did turn back to look at him, confusion glittered in those sparkling, shattered, jade-coloured eyes.

"And yet you did," she said in a whisper.

"And yet I did."

He went to tell her then who he was. Who cared if she thought he was crazy, if it would unlock her soul's memories. He would do it. But when those memories were unlocked, she might think that he was standing in her way, and he found – thanks to Aphrodite's influences – that he didn't want Amara thinking of him in that manner. It clawed at a primal part of him.

It was only in this moment, on the precipice of knowledge, on the impact of seeing her, that he realised just how clever the goddesses had been. If he was to protect Amara from their onslaught, he couldn't simply reveal what he knew, because she would now just think it was some elaborate excuse. He was going to have to find another way to do it.

She slid her hand away from his at his silence. Before he could take it back, they were interrupted.

"Amara, you ok, love?" Alice boomed from the doorway that led out into the kitchens and the back entrance.

Amara abruptly stood.

"Sorry, Alice ... let me just finish up."

Alice shook her head. "Ah, nah hen, leave it until tomorrow. You and your ... friend head on off now so I can lock up." There was a glint in Alice's eye that said she'd wanted to say more and was only holding back, as her boss, to spare Amara any embarrassment. Amara kept her head bowed as she ducked behind the counter to grab her bag and jacket.

Prometheus frowned. He wouldn't have expected a former priestess, particularly of Athena, Artemis, and Aphrodite, to be so meek with another woman. Men, he could understand, given what the goddesses had subjected Amara too. But still, they tended to pick their priestesses with more backbone. He worried that the fear had begun to seep a little deeper into Amara's bones, into the depth of her being, altering her on a fundamental level while he'd been gone. After all, nothing good had ever come from being in the human world for long. It was why he had given them the lifespan they had.

Then Amara threw him a look he couldn't decipher. One full of hurt and pain and ... something else.

"Don't come back, ok?"

So she had a backbone after all.

But before he had a chance to respond to that heartbreaking statement, which revealed the depth of the cut he'd caused, she walked out the door without him.

CHAPTER XXII

Aphrodite had asked him to make sure that Amara and Prometheus' union bore fruit. She had stoked the flames, she told him. Now it was simply a matter of letting inhibitions get the better of them. But after leaving his sisters, Dionysus had begun to hatch a plan of his own.

Always, Tyche managed to belittle him ever since she rebuffed his advances. To make him out like he wasn't good enough for her because he was merely the enabler of others' plans, that he never had the balls to take care of anything himself, that he wasn't man enough for her.

Well, her chance would be a fine thing. For what would Tyche's mother say if, after their priestess drove herself to subconscious abandon, Amara chose to end her life instead? What would the Goddess of Ill and Fair Fortune have to say for herself then? If he was merely an enabler and she the greater executor of plans?

That she would pick that stoic Titan Prometheus over his company was baffling too. What did she see in a man that had no sense of play? He was always so serious about everything. All doom and gloom and premonitions that stopped the fun of the humans in the first place. The fact his plan would hinder the Titan as well as Tyche in the eyes of his sisters was an even bigger incentive. So they would lose the priestess; it was no matter. There were plenty of other priestesses to choose from in Olympus. This opportunity to stick it to the goddess who had turned him down was too ripe to miss.

Tonight, while the priestess licked her wounds in a bottle of wine, Dionysus would make sure there were no boundaries inhibiting her from taking that final step off the precipice. After all, Aphrodite hadn't specified *which* inhibitions he had to lower.

Implication was a cunning mistress.

CHAPTER XXIII

A mara had thought that the busyness of the day had done the trick, until Theo had shown up. The minute she was home, too exhausted to cook or do anything other than plonk herself in front of the TV with a show that she wasn't really watching, her thoughts started to intrude on her again.

Why had Theo shown up today of all days? Had he seen her last night? What had Kiaria said to Alice? Would she lose her job even though she worked so hard today? God, had Alice known today? Had John said more had happened than it actually had?

She was starting to get an onset of a headache that she undoubtedly deserved, but her tastebuds craved more than water. So Amara wandered into the kitchen. She found an unopened, dusty bottle of wine that had been sitting at the back of the liquor cabinet no one in the house really used and grabbed the corkscrew. She twisted and pulled until she heard that satisfying 'pop' and the sweet sound of the first glug as the wine began to fill the glass. She drank it steadily, a slight dribble of red liquid escaping out the corner of her mouth in her haste, until the pangs of hunger disappeared and her head felt woozy.

At least those damn intrusive thoughts weren't bothering her anymore. She went to refill her glass and settled in to watch whatever mind-numbing thing was on the screen. As long as it would keep her thoughts off how good Theo had looked, smelled, felt ... that look of pity in his eyes that said he cared. She'd been *fine*.

One glass turned into another, and another.

By midnight, two bottles of wine and half a bottle of whisky down, the headache had returned. Rising unsteadily to her feet, she stumbled into the small bathroom across the hallway. Opening the medicine cabinet hard enough that it thwacked her in the forehead, she stumbled backwards.

"Ow." She rubbed at the place that was sure to bruise.

Blinking her eyes open, she began to scrounge around, looking for anything to take the edge off a headache that had just got infinitely worse.

"Paracetamol will do the trick." She hiccupped and murmured to herself.

That was the last thing she remembered before waking up in the bright lights of a hospital bed.

She'd never been in a hospital before, but this one didn't seem like the ones she'd seen on TV. For starters, it seemed to be a private room, with curtains on the window to her left and against the window at the foot of her bed. There was also a chest of drawers with a vase full of sunflowers at the foot of her bed. The room smelt nice, not at all like disinfectant. The only reason she knew she was in a hospital of any kind was because she was in a gown with a plastic tag around her wrist noting her full name and the time she had been checked in: 1 a.m.

Holding the hand that was attached to that braceleted wrist was a dishevelled Theo, whose bloodshot eyes said he hadn't slept at all. Not that Amara felt like she'd slept. Her head was heavy and groggy, her throat drier than sandpaper. Her stomach and ribs felt bruised. She felt more like she'd been beaten up rather than taken care of.

"Wh—" Amara tried to clear her throat and felt like shark skin was shredding her vocal cords. Theo lifted an ice chip to her lips, which she gratefully accepted, letting the cold water soothe her, before trying again. "What happened?"

Theo's eyes glanced back down. He couldn't even look at her.

"I know you said to not come back, but I wasn't going to abandon you when I'd emotionally ambushed you like that. That's on me. All this is on me. You hear me?"

"What are you talking about?"

His calloused thumb began stroking her own and it reminded her of hours earlier, in the café, still as equally soothing in gesture as it was irritating in texture.

"When I came by, the door was unlocked. When there was no answer, I was worried. And when I found you in the bathroom barely breathing ... I had no choice but to call the ambulance. They brought you here, pumped your stomach and are currently rehydrating you." Theo pointed with his free hand to the IV drip on the other side of Amara's bed that she hadn't even noticed.

"Oh God," Amara hung her head and tried to pull back her hand to hide her face in shame but Theo wasn't letting go.

"It's on me, my love, not you. Never you. I should have never left you to do this alone."

Amara didn't understand what he meant, her brain still foggy. She continued to refuse to look at him until he cupped the side of her head in one of those huge hands and stroked her hair.

"It was my fault. I won't abandon you again, ever."

A tear slid down her cheek. "Don't make promises you can't keep," she whispered as she turned her head away and fell back into a dreamless sleep.

CHAPTER XXIV

P rometheus had proven true to his word. He had wooed Amara with trips to all the local haunts initially, walking her back through their short history together. Reinforcing the memories. He had even taken her to the tartan shop that specialised in clans of old, only for the pair of them to find it had been closed for several months.

It had been a ploy, he admitted to himself. An easy out for him if Amara could discover her lineage for herself. And while she had been disappointed, Amara had still remained hopeful.

"There'll be other stores and answers out there somewhere. I have faith," she told him gently, taking his hand and leading him away from the empty storefront.

It reminded him of what she had told him the first time they had met, when she'd still been in her immortal form. Her resilience, her level of faith, after all the goddesses ... after what *he* had put her through, despite the fact her alchemy continued to elude her, floored him. The fact that she had also given him a chance to prove himself, hesitant as she was that he meant it, told him that she wanted to believe him a man worthy of her faith. *He* wanted to believe himself worthy of her.

Everyone who had become acquainted with Amara's world soon became acquainted with him too, particularly the regulars at the café. The mothers with their prams swooned over him, though he never offered them more than a courteous smile, his eyes clearly for Amara. Rhonda and Bessie cooed over him too, and for them he would make time to sit with them as they regaled him with stories of their youth. When he would finally excuse himself, always after a respectable amount of time, they would turn to Amara and remark on what a wonderful man he was, which always caused her to smile. As if she was not aware.

"Oh, dear, we forgot to tell you," Bessie said one day as Prometheus and Amara had joined their table. "We showed that tartan of yours to one of the historian enthusiasts in our prayer circle and she recognised it!"

Prometheus and Amara both sat up to attention. Amara leaned forward expectantly.

"Did she know where it was from?"

"Yes, she did! She said it was old Caledonian. What did she say that was? Oh yes, what the ancient Greeks called Scotland. She said your lineage must be of the ancestors of old."

"Oh," Amara replied, a look of puzzlement on her face. Prometheus could tell it hadn't been the answer she was expecting. In fact, it just left more questions.

"Of course, there's not much left on the knowledge of the ancestors before the ancestors ..." Rhonda chimed in, oblivious to Amara's reaction. But Prometheus knew well what it was like to be of ancestry forgotten.

"If there are more questions there will be more answers," he told her, reading those questions in her eyes.

"You're right," she said, shaking off the disappointment and smiling brightly. It didn't quite reach her eyes but the two ladies didn't notice. They were too busy cooing over how well matched Theo and Amara were.

Prometheus kept his eyes on Amara though. And he kept his eyes out for signs that the gods and goddesses were interfering again. But, as if they sensed him watching, they were nowhere to be found. Perhaps they now knew he was watching out for them. Perhaps they did not want to anger the one rule breaker who'd dared defy Zeus and lived to tell the tale. Even a Titan's reputation could make him a larger-than-life legend in their eyes. He was vigilant, keeping Amara close enough to know that she was wanted but at arm's length in case he got swept up in whatever sick game Aphrodite and Athena had decided to play next. It was clear to him that the two had, at some point, decided to use him. If they wanted to play a game of covert chess with human pawns, he would beat them at their own game. They would not be using Amara.

But as the weeks passed and the cool kiss of autumn pressed herself deeper into the streets of Edinburgh, Prometheus began to believe that Aphrodite had truly thought that true love would keep Amara safe. Still, something in the back of his mind nagged at him. How could they keep Amara safe and yet still do the Fates' bidding?

That night, at Kiaria's, a bottle of red wine lay breathing between them. All three glasses on the oak coffee table were full. Kiaria sat cross-legged, innocently, in purple and black splashed yoga pants and a matching loose-fitting black top, on the two-seater grey sofa. Prometheus was on a brown beanbag closer to the TV, which was currently off. Kiaria, despite her love for conversation, only liked one sound at a time and it was usually the sound of her own voice. Prometheus' legs spread to accommodate Amara between them, both of them facing Kiaria. Between them was the coffee table. There were already three empty bottles of the same brand of wine sitting by the recycling bin.

From what he gathered, the pair had fallen out. But when Prometheus had appeared on the scene once again, Kiaria had smiled sharply and forgiven Amara. Amara naively called it a misunderstanding, but Prometheus was no fool. He hadn't missed the glint of Kiaria's canines that said she smelt fresh blood and bathed in it.

She reminded him of Eris, Ares' sister, as she trailed her sword through eerily quiet battlefields stained with blood, her bare feet squelching on the torn-out organs of men and licking her tongue across the bloodied blade. A memory he would never forget. He found Kiaria's fickleness was as distasteful as Eris' bloodlust.

He would sooner prick Amara's skin with a pin before he entrusted her to this woman, but Amara appeared to like her. Then again, Amara was too soft once someone was under her defences. As if she was responsible for them once they were under those tortoiseshell-like barriers she put up.

"You really think humans have no free will?"

Kiaria had decided to engage him in a heated debate since the first bottle had been opened.

"That's not what I'm saying," he countered. "I'm saying the way they are wired only allows for so *much* free will."

"So what ... we're puppets?!" Kiaria wasn't buying it.

"No ... we're just wired a certain way."

They had been debating this one for the last hour and a half and were still coming back to the same point.

"Perhaps," Amara interrupted, the most sober of them all, "we should move on to another topic."

"I quite agree," Prometheus said. There was a brief pause.

"So *Theo*," Kiaria smiled. Prometheus did not appreciate the tone. Perhaps a change of conversation had not been the smartest idea.

"We've known each other, what? Two months now? And I haven't had the chance to ask ... what *are* your intentions with Amara?"

Prometheus grinned a boyish grin. One no one often saw on his face. The only other times he had smiled like this was when Amara had said something playful or when he didn't think she was looking.

"To make sure she's happy."

"And Amara, are you happy?" Kiaria asked.

"Of course I am." Amara stroked the jean-clad outer calf of Theo's leg that was wrapped around her. Whether it was to soothe him or her, he couldn't say. But it soothed something in him to have her touching him like this.

"For now, sure. But you can't want to work your entire life in Aunt Alice's café?" Kiaria pushed.

Amara shrugged. "I don't see anything wrong with doing service work."

Prometheus' legs clenched.

"There's something quite humbling about it," Amara continued. "You really get to know humanity, you know?"

"Well ... you couldn't pay me enough to keep doing it," Kiaria said, downing the rest of her glass before reaching for the wine bottle and pouring the dregs in. Sighing, she swung her legs over the sofa and rose. She had quit two weeks ago when John had left for a "real" job.

"That's the last of the wine. Let me see what else we have."

As Kiaria sashayed off into the kitchen, Amara squirmed and turned to face him. It was only when she began looking at him in concern that he realised his face had turned to granite, a large deep groove across his brow.

"Hey, is everything ok?"

"What did you mean when you said you get to know humanity?"

"Well ..." Amara settled back into his chest, burrowing herself closer to him. "For one, you can tell who has worked in hospitality before. They don't treat you like a servant but a person. They tend to be more patient, kinder, less demanding."

"And the ones who haven't worked in a café or the like before?"

"Tend to be more troublesome." Amara laughed.

"Has anyone been giving you trouble?"

"Just a couple of the snooty old biddies and a couple of judgemental mums. Nothing you need to worry about." Again, she reached out to stroke his leg. The gesture didn't soothe him as it had before.

"What is it?"

"You came here looking for answers, which you still don't have, but now you seem content to just be a waitress. Are you sure you're happy?"

If she truly was happy, he would be. He would keep her safe, especially from the antics of the goddesses. The rest of humanity could be damned now. He knew it would hurt, losing all those souls. It would tear out a part of him, but that part would heal ... eventually. It would be nothing, he knew, nothing compared to losing Amara.

If she wasn't happy, if the soul of the priestess was starting to wake up ... would she realise who he was? Would she be mad at him from keeping her from her moira? Would she push him away? Would he lose her? He couldn't abide that thought. Not now. Not now that he knew her.

"Just a waitress? Ouch." Amara's eyes uptilted in hurt. *Shit.*

"That's not what I meant. It's the wine ... forgive me?"

Amara gave him an assessing look, then nodded.

"Found it!" Kiaria walked back in holding another bottle of wine in the air triumphantly, the glass glistening off the kitchen light. On reading the room, she lowered the bottle.

"And I am going to take this off to bed with me ... I'll see you star-crossed lovers in the morning."

Amara glanced at the clock that hung above the armchair. "She's right. It's late. We should get going."

Prometheus didn't say anything but released Amara from the prison of his legs as she unfolded and rose languidly, like a cat stretching. Occasionally she did this, made movements that made her appear regal, and he was wracked with guilt again that he hadn't told her the truth. But what good would it do now? Until he figured out how to get her to transmute the fear that coiled tighter around her bones every day till she seemed frozen in a perpetual human loop of servitude, until he helped her overcome it, revealing her true heritage would simply be presenting her with her death warrant – a sure-fire way for the fear to eat her alive faster. He wouldn't do it.

He held hands with her the entire way back in the taxi. Penance he would willingly pay as her touch continued to burn into him.

When he moved to release her hand as they pulled up to Amara's house, she tugged at him, hard enough that he complied and slid across the slippery vinyl seats and exited with her. They both watched as the black cab disappeared off into the distance.

Prometheus had drunk his fair share of wine that night, considerably more than Amara, but he wasn't as drunk as she thought he was. Gods had a different metabolic constitution. Everyone knew that, even if they didn't believe in them anymore.

He looked down to Amara, her hand still clasped in his, saw the invitation in her eyes. The memory of last time hounded him but he was still a man. His cock twitched.

"Are you sure?" He needed to be certain. It had still only been a matter of months since her assault.

"I'm sure," she whispered, breaking his mental chastisement.

"We will stop if you ..."

Amara pressed a small finger to his lips. "Please don't ruin this," she whispered.

Her confirmation and admonishment pulled at something low in his gut, and whether it was that, the wine, or the way she looked at his lips, the last of his restraint shattered. He cupped her cheeks and kissed her. A full body kiss that had her pressing the full length of herself into his chest. Breasts crushed to him, he pushed one thigh between her own and she melded perfectly onto him. One of his hands flew down to her arse, cupping her firmly onto his thigh until she began rubbing against it needily. She moaned in the back of her throat as he thrust one of his hands into her hair, angled her head and deepened the kiss.

Eventually, Amara put her hand on his chest and he had just enough semblance of reasoning to pull back and allow them to gulp in breaths of fresh night air.

"Upstairs," Amara whispered.

"Yes."

She led him through the wooden door that creaked and into a sparse hallway, where a sideboard hosted a tangled, thirsty plant that almost touched the floor, a host of unopened mail and a tray of keys. Amara placed hers in the tray gently, pushed a finger to her lips to indicate her house mates were likely home and sleeping, given the number of keys in the dish, and they proceeded up the stairs on almost silent feet – Prometheus was heavy after all – until they reached the top of the stairs and turned immediately to the door on the left.

It was a small room, with the bed immediately to the right of the doorway and pushed against a cream wall. Opposite was a small bookshelf that was home to a few books Amara had picked up, a collection of crystals, bird feathers framed in a fan-like shape and a pot of potpourri. Prometheus smiled. If Amara had no inclination of her heritage, she really was being obtuse about it. Opposite the bed was a small wooden dresser that had a matching wooden vanity mirror leaning at an angle. He watched Amara's reflection as she made quick work of taking out her earrings and shaking her hair out, loose curls bouncing around her head ... before turning to him.

Part of his mind still functioned as his knees hit the back of the bed and he decided to sit. To let Amara take charge. To make sure she was comfortable throughout. Taking her cue from him, she immediately straddled him.

Her foot hooked around his left calf and began to rub up and down against his jeans. Underneath the hair on his legs, the friction of Amara's movements, made heat travel up his legs. Her hips began to make the same small movement against his groin. Groaning, he curled his hands back into her hair, and kissed her like a drowning man craving air. Amara made a needy little meowl in the back of her throat. His hands travelled down to her waist and under her jumper before his dark eyes snapped open and bored into hers.

"Yes?" He wanted to make sure she was with him, all the way.

"Yes," she said, breathless.

Making quick work of the jumper and blouse buttons underneath, with surprisingly nimble fingers given their size, he flicked them both to the ground, one hand cupping around her bare waist, barely grazing the black scrap of fabric that sat precariously below it. Amara rose to take off the remainder of her clothing, leaving her clad in only a black lace bra and underwear. Prometheus let out a dark groan.

Leaning forward, he pressed a kiss to her navel. Amara leaned her head back, goosebumps exploding the length of her body. Pulling her back down onto his lap, Prometheus' lips made their way back up her neck. He felt the rabbit of her pulse as his teeth grazed, slowly, gently at first, over it.

She moaned. *Good.*

Having kept one hand curved around her hip, he tugged at it, encouraging her to wrap her legs around him and begin those little needy hip movements again. She did. He groaned deeper. Those little movements of hers would be the undoing of him. Noticing this, Amara flashed him a small, satisfied smile and began to pick up the pace.

On her third upward thrust he took advantage, flipping her onto her back, being careful not to press the heavy weight of him onto her or reach for her arms or wrists.

"Still with me, princess?"

Amara nodded, biting her lip.

Prometheus cupped her cheek, lowered himself for a kiss, his longer hair now falling over his forehead as he did so, before his lips began to make their way down the centre of her body.

At the barrier of black lace, he hooked one calloused finger underneath them.

"I like these."

"You do?" The question was a careless one and Prometheus grinned against her thigh. This was the way he wanted her to feel. Carefree.

Tugging the scrap of black material away from her thighs, he made quick work of his own clothes before settling back over the top of her. Her leg hooked around him once again, and she sent him a look of challenge, as if to say, *what are you waiting for?* The leg around him squeezed, urging him towards her entrance. Still, he didn't move.

His weight was braced on his forearms on either side of Amara. Her nails clawed into his biceps as she thrust her hips up at him in demand. But he didn't want to rush this, rush her. He would savour her. Make her feel like the most delectable treat. Let her know that she was adored, her body worshipped in this act. He wanted to undo all the harm she had ever been forced to feel when it came to this intimacy. He wanted to earn her trust. To have her feel so safe and held that she would melt into him.

So he nuzzled at her neck again, biting gently at the curve between her neck and her delicate shoulder. She shuddered, her hand moving at once into his hair, but she didn't push him away. He continued to nuzzle as he played with her breasts, squeezing one of the small mounds before rubbing the nipple between his forefinger and thumb. Her grip in his hair tightened. He pinched her nipple. A gasp escaped her lips.

He looked up at her to check that she was still with him. Her eyes were hooded but they were very much on him, watching what his fingers were doing.

"Harder? Or softer?" he asked, demonstrating with her nipple as he did so. It was important that she make the decisions here. To know she was in control, though it was costing him every ounce of his strength to not lose his own.

"Harder," she said, her voice husky.

He obliged, this time using his mouth, his tongue and his teeth on the other nipple. Amara arched her back as he sucked deeply, moaning breathlessly as he did so. When he was sure she was on the precipice, he released it. Bowing her back down into the bed, he kept his hands on her breasts as his head made its way down to between her legs. Only then, when he was positioned at her entrance did he let his hands wander down and grip at her thighs, making sure to keep them at either side of his head. Glancing up, he saw she had moved onto her elbows to watch him.

Uncoiling one hand from her thigh, he moved it between her legs and pushed one finger in. Slow and deep. Then he withdrew. And again. By the third time, she was making small little circles with her hips and a needy moan in the back of her throat. He inserted a second thick finger. She stretched to accommodate him, the moan escaping her mouth this time, the breathy sound making him painfully harder. It wasn't enough.

Removing his fingers, he replaced them with his tongue and felt Amara buck against him. Taking long, slow, cavernous licks, he worked his way up to her clit, and flicked his tongue out over it. Amara bucked harder. Placing his whole mouth against her, he sucked and teased at her clit as his fingers went back inside her. Pumped once, twice. Circled that rough little spot on the inside that he'd designed to bring humans the ultimate pleasure and groaned as she finally let the pressure of the orgasm wash over her and onto his fingers.

Limp in a way that suggested she was satisfied, Prometheus moved back up her body, taking his time to feel every dip and valley of her skin as her breathing returned to normal. He skimmed her thighs, her belly, her breasts, before his hand curved around her neck and he took her lips in a deep kiss that she lazily returned. When they broke from the kiss, she opened her eyes and glanced down at their bodies.

"Are you planning on doing something about that?" she asked, a small smile flirting on her face.

"Witch," he growled back playfully.

He settled himself over her and between her legs, his weight once again braced on his forearms. He began to move slowly, his chest hair rubbing against her breasts. Amara parted with a moan against his lips. She was slick already. He barely had to push before he was so deep inside her he could feel her internal muscles pulsating on him. Groaning, he slid out slowly – the release, one of pleasure and pain intertwined exquisitely – before returning home to her. It was a slow, rhythmic build, one that had her panting with need, but he heard no complaints. Only soft moans that got higher and breathier the closer she came to surrendering again.

This time, when she spasmed around him, her legs shaking and her hands clawing desperately at the tangled white sheet beneath them, his false name on her lips, he let out a guttural groan of his own and joined her as the feeling of ecstasy sucked them both under.

....

The nightmare that night was a particularly bad one. Prometheus knew she'd been having nights of bad sleep. She'd told him that she still woke up in night sweats sometimes. Tonight, she tossed and turned in the sheet, one minute cuddled against him for protection whimpering as she did so. The next, her limbs pushed against him as if to force him away. Beads of sweat dripped down her forehead and every time he tried to wipe them away and brush her hair back, she fussed. But still she did not wake. Then, when Prometheus had thought she'd finally settled, she began to speak in her sleep.

"There never was a plan. You're liars, all of you. You know nothing. None of you do. You can't even see it, how far away from humanity we exist ... they are doomed. There is no redemption. Don't you see? You speak of love and war, justice and chastity, romance and wisdom as if they are each separate entities. But you put all of them within one human body. It is too much to bear. The burden is too great. Even I can feel this human body cracking under the pressure. You gave them voices but no valve. You, the wise one, didn't even see it coming ..."

Amara sighed heavily, as if she was resigned to her fate as her hair tickled against her nose. This time when Prometheus went to tuck it behind her ear, she let out a small smile and burrowed deeper into the cream white pillow. Then her whole body seemed to sigh as she settled into a deep sleep.

Prometheus, meanwhile, stared at her in concern, one hand propping up his head. Who had she been talking to? Athena? That would be the wise one she mentioned. But she'd also said love and chastity ... perhaps Aphrodite ... and had Artemis been there too? Surely she wouldn't have spoken to her patrons in such a manner? Insubordination like that could see you strung up for an eternity of pain. Though, of course, if what Amara said was true ... she was telling them that they had already condemned her when they sent her here. And if there wasn't a plan, if humanity truly was doomed ...

A dull ache formed in the crater in his chest that Amara had smashed through, as his foresight returned with unrelenting force. It played out perfectly in his mind, the low tug in his gut confirmation that it would come to pass. The weight of the knowledge rocked him, until he crushed Amara's soft body against his harder one. As if he hadn't already tied his fate to hers.

She made a noise of complaint when he held her too hard and he, unwillingly, loosened his grip.

He now understood the Fates' hand. Aphrodite's task. His role. How it all came together perfectly. It could still work. There was hope yet. He knew what he had to do.

First, he must speak with Zeus.

CHAPTER XXV

He had given himself a week before he told Amara he would be away on business for a while. Logic had dictated that he was pacing himself, but even he knew that was a lie. He wanted more time with her. He wasn't ready to leave just yet. That selfish desire quietly told him not to rush. That desire outweighed the voice in his head that told him to use his knowledge to immediately solve Amara's problem ... not that she remembered her sleep talking when he'd questioned her about it.

A week was nothing in the scheme of things, he reasoned to himself. Plus it allowed him to plan how he would tackle Zeus' ego enough to get him onboard with Prometheus' plan. He'd learnt from the last time. This time he *had* to make sure it was the God of God's idea.

"And who needs your crafts this week?" She'd teased playfully in bed the morning before he'd left for Olympus.

"My main patron."

"Patron? Are we living in the Renaissance era?"

Prometheus had scratched at his stubble, trying to think of a better way to describe Zeus but the only other words he had for his long-term friend were decidedly too brash and rude. Instead, he placed a soft kiss on her head.

"I'll be back before you know it."

"I know," she said softly, giving him a gently admonishing look, her eyes filled with what he was hopeful was returned love.

She tugged him down for a proper kiss. He allowed her tongue to tease the edges of his mouth until he coaxed her lips open and flicked his tongue into hers. He angled his jaw, deepening the kiss, loath to ever let it end. Eventually he pulled back. He had to.

"I'll be fine," she told him. "Go."

And so here he was, wandering the dusty track of the mountains that would lead onto a spectacular field of meadows, still ripe in greenery. It used to be ripe with maidens too that Zeus often chased when his wife, Hera, wasn't looking. Prometheus was sure he'd find him here today. He was right.

"Prometheus, old friend!" Zeus boomed across the field, making large strides towards him and enveloping him in a hug that suggested he'd forgotten the two of them had fallen out. Given the number of tasks on the King of Olympus' to-do list, this was entirely possible. Given his ability to hold grudges, it was not. Zeus could be a mercurial character ... but today, it seemed, he swung in Prometheus' favour.

"How are my humans? I assume that's where you've been all this time? Hera has been asking after you, you know.

Telling me I should invite you to dine with us. I told her I would if you'd show your bloody rugged face ... and here you are. So tell me, how are they?"

Another common trait of Zeus' – to not let another get a word in edgeways. It was understandable. He'd been a boisterous young boy and an upstart of a young man. Not abandoned per se but certainly left to his own devices for most of his youth, Zeus had carried that penchant for being the centre of attention ever since.

"They're ... as well as can be expected, Lord."

"Oh don't you start with your doom and gloom now! And stop with the formalities. Our squabble is finished now that you have served your time. Look, Apollo has set the sun high in the sky today! Why not come out on a hunt with me? Fresh air running through your lungs will shake off any tendrils of those pesky thoughts running through your mind."

Clearly someone had played a hand in letting Zeus think his time had been served and that there was to be no further consequence. Prometheus wondered if that had been Athena or Tyche's doing.

"No, Zeus, I need to speak with you."

"We can speak as we hunt."

Prometheus knew that tone. There was no room for debate.

The hunt ran from the afternoon to the early hours of the evening. Zeus set a punishing pace, even for a Titan such as Prometheus. Sometimes Zeus partook in a sneaky hunt, but today he was clearly feeling boisterous, bellowing out across the fields, giving the heifers plenty of warning to scarper. Zeus laughed at the thrill of the chase, and the two gods jested with each other all afternoon about who would catch the prize. Of course, it was always to be Zeus. He caught the biggest heifer and killed it quickly and cleanly, before the pair of them carried it back by its legs to the fire pit outside the palace Zeus and Hera called home. Prometheus proceeded to skin it and fillet off the meat. They would eat it that night.

"I'll get Dionysus to join us and bring some wine."

"Wait, Zeus. I would speak to you first. Alone," Prometheus stressed. Zeus sighed wearily and for the first time Prometheus detected age in his sigh.

"Very well, what troubles you so? You've been badgering for my ear all day."

Prometheus paused, composing himself, before speaking.

"Athena approached me some time ago with concerns over the humans."

"Missing us, are they?" Zeus chortled, but his heart wasn't in it. The humans, once his most cherished possession, were now abandoned like an old toy a child no longer wished to play with. Instead, he stared at the meat, practically salivating though it had barely begun to char.

"Zeus, they are dying."

That got his attention. His eyes, a cobalt blue so painful they could pierce your soul, snapped to Prometheus. Oh make no mistake, it wasn't because Zeus cared about the humans. Well, he did. It was … complicated. Prometheus knew Zeus had asked him to make the humans in his image after all, so he loved them. It was just that, sometimes, Zeus didn't particularly like what he saw in the mirroring they offered him. Perhaps Prometheus had been *too* accurate in his portrayal. Perhaps that had had a little influence over his sentencing too.

About to bite out a retort, Prometheus quickly continued. He must play this right and there was no room for interruptions.

"Athena was right in her concerns. I can see why she is favoured."

Something flickered behind Zeus' eyes and Prometheus imagined Athena's mother, who had turned into a snake and inhibited Zeus' mind after he'd swallowed her, was listening also. Zeus paused for a moment, cocking his head, before offering an amused smile that held an inch of cruelty.

"It's not like you of all people to give platitudes, Prometheus." Zeus' lips tilted up further.

Prometheus had been sure that praise would have been important to both Athena's mother and the boy within Zeus who had never had anyone else to truly play with and praise him. Well, apart from that goat-like nanny of his with hairs on her chin, who no one seemed to count.

He continued carefully, "I do so because I now share her concerns. After spending time in the human realm, I can see Athena is right ... your humans are in trouble."

Zeus waved his hands in a gesture of ill concern and returned his attention to the fire pit. "I'm sure she will take care of it."

Here it goes.

"Her plan is failing, my Lord."

Zeus merely hummed unconcernedly.

Prometheus tried a different tack.

"While the statues of you remain, there is no adoration towards you like there once was."

Prometheus began to see a thick vein in Zeus' neck pulsate.

"And instead of heeding your lessons of decadence, they have begun to sacrifice themselves. Albeit in a more ... discreet manner, so as not to capture your attention."

Zeus' head snapped back to him. Everyone in Olympus knew Zeus had specifically forbidden the humans to sacrifice themselves before Hera's ruling had taken effect. He had told them he found the act itself repugnant. His eyes bored into Prometheus. Cold and calculating they were much like a predator measuring another predator of a different species.

"They dare defy me? Again? Are you certain?"

"Without question. But there must be a reason why the Fates turned to Athena." A little pandering would not hurt Prometheus' cause. "Perhaps there is still something that can be done."

Zeus shrugged. "I could simply ask Poseidon to wipe them all out with another flood. Problem solved. Now can we eat?"

"You would really put yourself through this whole sorry charade again?"

"Come now ... you enjoyed making them the first time, didn't you?"

"I did," Prometheus nodded in agreement while silently cursing him. "But I thought that there may be an even more ingenious plan for you to embark on."

"Oh?" Zeus turned the leg of the heifer with his bare hands, the heat of the fire doing nothing to scorch the God of Lightning, impatience thrumming through his blood.

"You could give the humans the gift of white fire."

Zeus paused for a moment before letting out a belly-aching laugh that roared through the heavens. He stopped when Prometheus did not join in.

"You would have me give them our knowledge?"

"Your humans are killing themselves. They have no idea what awaits them. All their science gives them is a sliver of information and they are exhausting themselves, their bodies, each other ... desperately trying to get answers."

"This never happened to the philosophers. Why don't they just listen to them?"

"The philosophers are a dying breed, mocked amongst their kind. Humanity has begun to fear what it does not know now we have left and they only trust what they can answer. They will kill themselves trying to get there."

Zeus was quiet for a moment. Prometheus knew Zeus understood the self-sacrifice he spoke of, but he could not tell if Zeus' silence was in contemplation or boredom.

"Would you really want to lose them?" Prometheus asked. "Remember the days when fair maidens would walk past you, offering coy looks?" He pressed on. "The thrill of the chase before they bowed down at your feet? The adoration they show that a nymph, Oceanid or fellow goddess will not?"

"No," Zeus said slowly.

"Imagine how much greater that adoration will be if they *know* how tiny and insignificant they are compared to you. It won't be like the old days where they knew about us, about you, from the beginning. It won't be a given. They consider themselves your equal now."

A dark, brooding grumble began to stir in Zeus' mouth.

"They'll fight you now. Wouldn't that make the chase so much sweeter, rather than the ones who give themselves so willingly here hoping to gain favour? Don't you miss when you had to trick them? Imagine the shock and awe they will feel when they realise that you grace them with their presence. Once they concede, they'll love and adore you, fear and worship you, obey your every whim in a way they never have before."

"Psychological warfare," Zeus mused. "Well, it does sound rather ... novel, after all this time."

"Psychological warfare is what they need," Prometheus agreed, as he handed Zeus the juiciest flank of meat. Zeus ripped the meat from the bone and began methodically chewing. When Zeus' smile began to turn to a frown, Prometheus pre-empted him.

"Hera need not know. I can take the task for you. Slip the fire into the hands of a select few. Replace the fire before anyone knows it was missing and let the humans' need for telling tall tales of legends naturally do the rest ..."

Zeus ripped another large chunk of meat off the bone with his teeth and swallowed while thinking.

"Well, I suppose no one is going to find it hard to believe that you offered the humans another gift of fire should we get caught."

Prometheus grunted in agreement.

"But naturally, I'll have to be seen as punishing you again for this if we do. Would you really put yourself through that again? Just for them? The humans?"

"Solitude was not so great a punishment for one like me. You and I both know that, my friend." Prometheus shrugged.

Zeus smiled at the informality and this time it appeared neither cunning nor cruel, malicious nor boisterous. It was golden. In that rare moment, he truly was the King of the Gods.

"Alright, you may give them the white fire my friend, but no one may know until it is done or else all hell will break loose."

CHAPTER XXVI

When night fell, Prometheus stepped out of his workshop in Olympus, dressed in the black and gold gilded armour Tyche had seen him working on the last time he was here. He hadn't known then what he was going to use it for, but one like Prometheus would never admit to being under the influence of one of the nefarious Muses. Many had invited themselves into his dreams ever since he met Amara. He was usually adept at ignoring them.

Unwilling to admit he was grateful for their interference this time, he stroked and surveyed his handiwork. It was made of the finest leather, rather than metal, given where he was going. It didn't even look like armour at all, more like a second skin. One that contoured to Prometheus' body, that allowed him freedom of movement and maximum protection against the heat. It also blended him so well into the night that even the glints of gold-threaded lining wouldn't be picked up by anyone, not even if he were to be followed by Zeus' eagle.

The road to where the fire was kept was a treacherous one, given how few ever climbed it. Indeed, Prometheus thought back to the only time it had been used – when he and Zeus had returned the fire after heating the furnace for the first humans.

Born of earth, water, air, and fire. The only species like it.

The climb began like any other in Olympus, simply a dusty road leading to nowhere. But as Prometheus pierced the cloud layer, the terrain became harsher. Craggy rocks jutted out and if you didn't know where to place your feet, you could cause a boulder to fall, a broken ankle if you fell into a crevice, or simply a slip that would have you tumbling down a jagged, rocky mountainside. Prometheus could afford none of these options. It wasn't that he couldn't feel pain, but because no one could know he was here.

Thankfully, being a man of his hands, he used most of his senses to feel his way up through the mountainside, relying on his memory to guide him up the least treacherous path to the white fire. Several hours had passed by the time he made it to the mouth of the cave and sweat was dripping down his temples, a fine sheen of perspiration covering the rest of his toned body. But, given his impeccable workmanship, the leather had not chafed but glided smoothly. Sweat didn't even cause it to squeak.

His forearms bulged as he used the weight of them to carry him up to the lip of the small cave. He knew it was the right one, for just beneath the lower lip was an olive branch, completely out of place in this terrain, precisely why he had left it there last time. Should he or Zeus have need to come up again, his foresight had foretold, he would use the olive branch as a guiding post. Sometimes his gift was useful.

Hoisting himself up by his leathered forearms, he crouched and crawled on his belly into the heart of the cave. There, at the back, was the white fire. The cave was much deeper than it appeared, the white fire a mere speck down a long, dark caved corridor devoid of light.

Prometheus wondered if this was what the humans meant when they said they saw 'a light at the end of the tunnel' when their human remains returned to Gaia. He wondered if some imprint of the fire that had branded them was etched into their DNA. Some ancient knowledge, some part of the fire crackled throughout them, longing to be reunited.

Reaching the back of the cave, he could feel the heat searing off the white fire. It crackled over the three branches. Those branches had come from the first tree Gaia had sprouted. The tree of knowledge, some had called it. It had transcended across all religions in some form or another. The burning bush, the tree of knowledge ... the humans had a multitude of stories for it. All true. All missing details. Funny, how they still argued over those details while missing the facts. It was the only tree that could contain the everlasting white fire that never burnt out. So he and Zeus had trimmed three branches, with Gaia's permission, and hidden the white fire here so the mortals and gods alike would never find it. Except now they needed it. Amara needed it.

Teeth gritted in determination, Prometheus reached in and grabbed one of the branches. Though it scorched his skin to do so – for God of Fire he may be but this was no normal fire – the agony was just about bearable with the leather protection. With the white fire in his grasp, he didn't have long to get back down the mountainside and into the human realm. Carrying the white fire would attract the attention of many should they see it. The way the white flame danced into purple, with glints of gold and blues and greens … it was unmistakable.

Making his way as carefully but as quickly as he could back down the mountain track, Prometheus paused only twice. Both times when he suspected he was being watched by something or someone. Luckily, there were plenty of large boulders to obscure him, and the fire, from view. Eventually he made it back down the mountain, through the still-sleeping Olympus before Apollo set the sun in the sky, and over the rainbow bridge provided by Iris.

The rainbow bridge – the connection between the heavens in Olympus the gods resided in and the Earth the humans inhabited. Separated only by the fact that the humans couldn't physically *see* the bridge. That would begin to change now.

For with the white fire, the humans would have access to all the same knowledge that the gods held. To look into the white fire was to burn away all hidden secrets. Any human who looked into it would have their memory restored … to the beginning of time. To when they were created. They would know exactly their role on Earth once more.

It was a dangerous gift. Not one that could be given to everyone. It would cause carnage and chaos in the wrong hands. But for Amara, it would unlock the memories she needed to be freed from a human prison and restore her alchemy. It was the only way. The challenges had failed, her alchemy lost. Even his love hadn't burnt away the fear that resided in her even now. *This* was the only way to save her. He just hoped that by presenting her with it he would redeem himself, for all the months of deception, in her eyes.

Prometheus stepped over the threshold, white fire in hand.

CHAPTER XXVII

"A mara ... Amara ..."

"Theo?" Amara muttered groggily, sitting up on one elbow while her other hand tried to rub sleep from her eyes haphazardly. The room was blurry as she blinked them open and for a moment she didn't realise where she was.

That's right, she thought. She had fallen asleep on the sofa in the communal living room again. She turned towards the sound of Theo's face and felt warmth stroke her face.

That's weird. Why had he lit a fire inside when autumn was still relatively warm this year?

Looking towards the grate, she saw that the fire was flickering a white gold. She shook her head, trying to clear the blur behind her eyes and see the flames as they were. It didn't work. Rubbing her eyes again, she stared. But the flames didn't change.

Turning to her right, she looked at him. There he was, his face strained in concern. She could have sworn he had aged in the time he had been away. Deep grooves bracketed his mouth and furrowed his brow. She traced them with her fingertips. They felt real enough.

She glanced back to the fire, which now had streaks of purple and gold flickering through it. She was definitely still dreaming. She must lay off the brandy, she reminded herself.

"Amara, are you listening to me? I need you to listen."

"Mmm," she murmured. The fire was so warm, the blanket so snuggly, the sofa beneath her spongy in its softness as she settled back down ...

"Amara!" A hard shake of her shoulders that stuttered her bones.

"What?!" she said, sitting bolt upright in alarm.

"I need you to listen to me carefully. I can't stay long."

"The dream is going to end soon," she rationalised to herself, nodding as she did so and sliding back down.

"Amara, this isn't a dream," he urged.

She cocked her head to one side. "Then why are you leaving? You know I don't like it when you leave." Tears began to traitorously leak out of her eyes.

Prometheus realised she must think she was still dreaming, for while she wore her heart on her sleeve, she did so unknowingly. She was never willingly vulnerable. To be so would be to admit to him that she ...

They didn't have time for this.

He needed to get Amara to see the fire and put it back before anyone on Olympus noticed something was happening in the human realm. No one need know he had brought the fire here. He could claim Aphrodite's plan had worked, that it had awakened Amara to her alchemy gifts once again.

Aphrodite would buy it, for she was vain like that, and no one would question her success for fear of facing her wrath. Amara could then teach the gifts and Zeus would get his way with the humans without realising Prometheus had tricked him. It could work, but Amara had to be willing.

He raised his hand to cup her cheek, but when tears continued to slide down them slowly, he wiped them with his thumb, brought it to his lips and sucked the droplet into his mouth.

"Amara, I'm here. You can feel me. See?"

Why was he here in the middle of the night if it wasn't a dream?

She watched his lips moving. The same lips that had kissed and sucked her tears away.

"I need you to look into the fire, Amara."

"Why?" she muttered, unimpressed with this dream Theo. He was demanding, whereas hers was not.

He contined to stare at her, hard, before gripping her shoulders.

"I can't tell you yet. I just need you to look. Can you do that for me?"

"Will you let me sleep if I do?"

Prometheus sighed, regretfully. For when she looked in the fire, she would never truly be asleep again.

"Yes, you can sleep afterwards," he lied.

"Ok then." Amara sat up in her dazed state, somewhere between consciousness and dreams, and stared into the fire.

It continued to flicker white gold. Meanwhile, the clearer Amara's vision got the more she couldn't believe what she was seeing. The gold and purple threads in the fire weren't just dancing; they were interacting with each other. Like two dancers that had known each other a lifetime, they came together and withdrew to a drumbeat that matched the timing of Amara's heartbeat.

She stood and walked closer to the fire, falling to her knees as she reached the hearth. Moving so he was behind her, one knee propped up and his weight leaning mainly on his left arm, Prometheus watched the fire with her.

As the threads entangled, Amara saw them become two figures. The purple thread was curvaceous, like a woman. The gold was upright, lean, like a man. It led the purple thread through the fire dance, and Amara got the distinct impression that she was watching the union of two people. At first she wondered if it was her and Theo, if he – the dream – was trying to tell her something. But then the threads of the flame began to tell a story without her prompting.

The purple thread lay horizontally across the fire while the gold thread covered her. Embers spat, causing Amara to jump. She shook her head, focused, and saw that the little embers had produced wisps of new threads. They were turquoise blue. Before Amara knew it, there were enough blue threads in the fire to weave together a scene.

"The birth of Earth," a breathy whisper said. She realised it was her voice.

The threads of the flame, as if they heard her, dispersed and began to weave together a new image. This time the golden thread took the shape of a bird and the purple the shape of a crown which then birthed twelve new threads.

Not all of them, Amara noticed, came from the purple thread but all of them had a tie to the gold thread. Until it looked as though the gold thread sat on the top of a mountain. As if the other threads had placed it there.

"Zeus and his children," Prometheus prompted, for the fire would only show Amara the knowledge she needed to know, no more, no less, of the history.

For some reason his words tugged deep in the recess of Amara's mind. She knew he was right. She didn't even turn to question him; she just kept watching.

The threads dispersed again and this time three purple threads appeared.

"What do you see?" he asked her.

"An owl, an arrow, and a woman." Amara said slowly, as the images became clearer, sharper to her eye.

"Athena, Artemis, and Aphrodite," he told her.

And then, a new thread appeared, crimson in colour. At first, it looked like a woman kneeling before all three goddesses before seeming to morph and become a small infinity symbol held in the goddesses' arms almost like ... a swaddled baby.

A single tear rolled down Amara's cheek as she watched the fire tell the story of her birth here on Earth. The lineage she had always wanted to know presented to her. It was a bittersweet gift, because with it came the realisation that she had been used for a task. Her life here on Earth held meaning, but not one that any human would wish on themselves.

She wasn't dreaming.

The fire had opened that trap door at the back of her mind that had kept her firmly cut off from her soul, and the memories came flooding back. Walking the fields, laughing as Artemis' hounds tried to catch butterflies in their teeth and brought her back dandelions instead. Tending to Athena's owls in the aviary. Collecting the rose petals and drawing the baths that Aphrodite had loved so much. And going to the temple to give thanks for her life in Olympus with her sisters, the other priestesses.

They had promised her glory for her gifts, and instead she had been *used. Hounded. Discarded when the plan didn't work. By those who had sworn to protect her. By those she had shown nothing but loyalty to.*

She remembered meeting Prometheus in Olympus. Even there he had been a man of legend. The one who had stood beside Zeus and fought with him in the Battle of the Titans. The elusive artist who had created humans but liked to keep himself to himself up in the mountains. To know him was to be invited to know him. There he had seemed older, wiser, more unreachable than any of the others. Yet here he was, his breath on the nape of her neck, his body so close to hers she could feel his body heat more intimately than the heat from the fire in front of her.

"Why?" she whispered.

He didn't pretend not to understand her meaning.

"I did it to protect you."

Another tear silently rolled down her cheek.

"Why not just tell me? Why now?"

There was a pause while Prometheus considered his words carefully.

"I wanted to, the minute I knew I'd found you. There would have been nothing easier than having you remember your lineage so that Hera could deem it to be considered meddling in the human realm and have you sent back to Olympus."

"But you didn't," she said softly.

"I didn't," he agreed.

"You used me."

Prometheus went to refute her claims immediately, only to pause. Because she was right. One thing he could never accuse the priestess of was being anything less than acutely emotionally intelligent. Instead, he could only match truth with truth.

"I fell in love with you."

At her silence, he continued.

"By the time I found you, the fear of humanity had already seeped below your human skin. I became terrified that if you were recalled to Olympus, or worse cast out without us solving this fear epidemic that taints the humans while in your human form, that it would curse you into an eternity of carrying it." *And that she would blame him for it.*

"Why tell me now though?" Amara still didn't have the heart to look at him. She still didn't want to look in those eyes of deepest brown and see regret in them, or knowledge of how her fate played out.

"The other night, in your sleep, you tried to send a message to the goddesses. You said their plan had no hope of succeeding. That there was no way to alchemise the fear in humans. You said it was impossible without a valve of some kind."

Amara sat quietly in contemplation.

"Giving you the knowledge of the gods was my last resort. It was the only way I could think to save you, to give you access to your alchemy, and know you'd not think me a madman."

"Zeus knows?"

"He knows enough."

The unspoken words sat between them and the enormity of what Prometheus had done stretched out like a chasm between them in the silence. She knew exactly what he wasn't saying. He had tricked Zeus, for her.

"Then you have cursed us both."

"I would rather spend eternity in the underworld doing Hades' bidding than watch you suffer here on Earth."

Finally, Amara turned and looked at him with a look that stripped him of his armour, his intellect ... and the earth shattered. In the depths of her eyes, he saw the finale to his foresight premonition he had missed in his haste before.

"You are a blind fool," she said quietly, as the knowledge of what was to become of them sunk into their bones. For she knew that even should she hope to share the knowledge, to teach the humans alchemy, there was no way Prometheus' actions would go unnoticed. Zeus had likely allowed him to merely think he was on board with the plan to see if the Titan had learnt his lesson, which clearly he had not.

That Titan went to cup her face, to tell her desperately what to do next, to kiss her one last time, when the sweet smell of rain snuck up on them, thunder rumbled and lightning cracked the sky.

CHAPTER XXVIII

The Moirai gathered in the silk room at the top of the old, abandoned church right below the bells. No one ever suspected that the Fates resided in a church and that was just the way they liked it. It was better to be undisturbed while they did this work.

There was one teardrop window in the room. It was surrounded by black brick, and a pair of old, dark wood slats – so dark as to look black – were open, giving the sisters a clear view of the blue sky beyond. The air swept in and the sunshine highlighted the motes of dust that swirled in the air in a downward spiral to the dusty floorboards. Those floorboards creaked with age as each sister took her place. Clotho by the loom, Lachesis on the other side to help tease the threads out, and Atropos standing behind her, watching over her shoulder, ready to cut.

A hum of energy surrounded the sisters as they began. The loom squeaked as if stretching awake, the tapestry resting heavily on Lachesis' knees. The air around them from the open window was fresh, sharp, but not as sharp as the breath both older sisters took as they watched Clotho reach for the white silk thread.

There had only been three times that thread had ever been chosen in the tapestry. Once, right in the beginning when the humans had been created and honed in the fire. The second time, far more recently, when they had known the actions Prometheus would take. Now, they found it picked up once again.

The sisters looked at each other. Stories in the tapestry had a way of being cyclic. It needn't be spoken amongst them that this could be the beginning of the end they had been so desperately seeking for the tapestry.

The hum continued as they quietly got to work. The white thread was quickly interlaced with the purple and gold threads, as the Fates had expected. But then something strange happened. Instead of the white thread engulfing the entire tapestry, Clotho picked up a caramel thread that was laced with filaments of gold. As the sisters watched and worked, an unmistakable profile began to take shape. As they worked, the face became an arm that carried the white fire of knowledge across the tapestry.

Lachesis cackled. "Oh, clever."

"What is it?" Atropos demanded.

"Do you remember why we set the priestess as a lost soul in Artemis' fields?"

"So that she was at one with nature," Atropos replied.

"And why we gave her the thirst to pursue lessons of love with Aphrodite and courage with Athena?" Lachesis asked.

"So that she would learn how to alchemise as a woman might. What does that have to do with the ... oh."

"Oh what?!" Clotho interrupted her sisters, also desperate to know.

"Don't you see, sister?" Lachesis said.

"Amara's alchemy is a skill but not her purpose. She was lost, so that she may recognise loss in others," Atropos added.

They began to trace her story in the tapestry. "She has learnt what she must in that time to help bring lost souls home to the truth of their nature, the love they deserve, the courage it takes to get them there. She has become a priestess for the souls who have lost their way – the humans. She was always supposed to be Prometheus' priestess."

Understanding began to dawn between all three of them. For if Amara was always to be Prometheus' priestess, then the white fire was simply another tool for her to complete her destiny. The priestess herself had never been the saviour for humanity. She had been the catalyst, the conduit. The reason Prometheus moved the white fire. Now the fire had been lit and it would spread, eradicating the fear, scorching the Earth to nourish the minds of those that Gaia made home for. The question was, would the humans survive it?

The crones continued weaving well into the night, the tapestry now lit by wall-mounted lights that offered a warm, yellow glow. They did not stop, desperate to see how it unfolded. They watched the priestess' actions become clearer in the tapestry. While Zeus' eagle escorted Prometheus back to Olympus, Amara had taken a candle to the white fire in the hearth and scurried away, hiding it in what appeared to be a cupboard.

Clotho picked up the next thread.

CHAPTER XXIX

P rometheus was escorted to Zeus and Hera's palace by an
eagle so large he could pick up Prometheus himself and
carry him back to Olympus if he had to. Instead, the bloody
bird decided to keep a discerning eye on him, squawking in
warning whenever it looked like Prometheus was not going
to follow the clear flight path of Zeus' pet. Eventually they
arrived, Prometheus dirty, parched, and exhausted from the
journey with no break. Exactly how Zeus intended him to be.

Like the last time he was here, he was escorted to the
courtyard, for the weather was still warm enough to eat
outside. Unlike last time, there was a hustle and bustle about.
The long stone table, which could seat all twelve Olympians,
was set in colours of deep ruby red laced with gold, gilded
utensils, goblets, and other finery. The nymphs fanned about
like mother hens, clucking as they laid the table. Raised by
Hera, they were matronly in their demeanour and dress,
with long gowns made of chiffon that covered all their
attributes and hair coiled back under maiden caps. Most

of them had learnt to avoid Zeus' gaze so as not to infuriate their mistress, and so they too ignored Prometheus, who appeared to be the only one present.

The table was laid for only three.

Taking one of the side seats at a nymph's request, for the head of the table was surely Zeus', Prometheus waited. The time walking here had given him a chance to clear his head after his summons from Zeus had been ... unmalleable. The time at the table gave him clarity to prepare for the calamity he knew was about to hit. Ever since Amara had looked him in the eyes, the words unspoken between them, his foresight had returned with a roaring vengeance. Now it prowled behind his eyes, cagey, pacing, desperate to get out.

Instead, his eyes tracked as Zeus made his way into the courtyard, followed shortly by ... Dionysus. Prometheus stood. Zeus didn't even acknowledge the formality with so much as a nod.

"Prometheus."

"My Lord." Despite the fact Zeus was not his Lord, it was the proper term for *occasions* such as this. And Prometheus made no mistake – this would be an occasion, for he couldn't understand why Dionysus was here unless he was to serve as a witness.

Both the men sat, Zeus at the head of the table and Dionysus opposite him.

The God of Wine produced a bottle and began to pour Zeus' cup first. In his eager haste, the wine sloshed over the rims of the goblets and onto the table.

"It is a new blend, gentlemen," he announced.

"What have you decided to call it?" Zeus asked, taking a sip before scowling at his goblet in displeasure. By the pinched look of his mouth, the grapes were far too tart for his liking.

"I don't name them; the humans do! I simply drink them and observe that their effects take hold as they should." A coy grin from the god. Many a baby had been sired thanks to Dionysus' input.

"And right you are, Dionysus," Zeus raised his own goblet again in a mock toast.

Prometheus sensed the trap and said nothing.

"Speaking of ... who is that delightfully enchanting human I've seen you hanging around with Prometheus?" Dionysus asked, taking a large gulp of wine before leaning back in his chair, balancing precariously on two legs.

"Yes, Prometheus," said Zeus darkly. "Why don't you tell us of this human woman it appears you have been spending all your time with?"

When he didn't answer, Dionysus continued digging. "She must be someone special. I've seen the way you two are together. Warm smiles shared over fire-breathing whisky, the odd nightcap. Why just the other night there was a rather heated discussion over a bottle of wine or three, wasn't that right?"

Prometheus wanted to kick the legs out from under the chair and send the god toppling backwards onto his sorry arse, where he belonged.

When the silence stretched on, Zeus growled. "You've been holding out on me, Prometheus. Come, I would have you tell us all about this woman who has captured your attention."

Prometheus had no intention of doing any such thing. It was already painfully apparent Zeus knew everything he needed to know, or at least he thought he did, in order to pass judgement. At that moment, Prometheus' thought of Jesus, a man named Judas, and a table laid for twelve.

He chose to answer the question with one of his own.

"Tell me, Dionysus, who bore the bloodline of Judas with a human lover thanks to my acts, how did you know?"

Dionysus stroked his wisp of a beard that still looked like bumfluff on his chin and shrugged. "I keep an eye on Tyche's proclivities. I found it rather interesting when she stopped going to visit your cabin."

Prometheus remained silent as he rocked back in his own chair observing his accuser.

"I've never known her Highness of Chance to ever bestow such favourable odds to anyone before as I have you," Dionysus continued.

"Perhaps that's because you forever skew her odds with your wine," Prometheus finally answered, giving him a pointed look.

Dionysus and Tyche had a ... complicated relationship. Given her influence, and Dionysus' penchant for not wanting any responsibility, there was once a time when the young god had wanted to woo the Goddess of Chance. However, true to form, Tyche had proven to be fickle ... stringing the young upstart along until revealing her hand, which had not swung in Dionysus' favour. Humiliated in front of the family, Dionysus had started taking his responsibilities a little more seriously from then on, often at the frustration of Tyche. It would likely be a cat-and-mouse game that would last for millennia, though Prometheus knew who he would place his money on. She would be pleased, he thought, to learn that he had finally learnt the lesson of loyalty over logic.

"What did you say this human woman's name was again?" Dionysus asked coyly.

Prometheus specifically hadn't mentioned her name. It shouldn't have been a problem. The gods often treated the humans as little more than toys; they certainly didn't care for names. But Dionysus had a bee in his bonnet, as the humans would say, that Tyche and he got on so well. And now Prometheus couldn't very well claim not to know her name, not given the amount of time he'd spent with her. Then there was the fact that he had always prided himself on learning the humans' names. It was a point he had been teased for relentlessly in Olympus in the past.

"Amara," he said eventually.

"Amara ... Amara. Now where do I know that name from? Hold on a moment. Isn't that the name of the priestess Athena and Aphrodite have been arguing over the last few months?"

Prometheus stared at him.

"How the hell did you know about that?" he growled.

Dionysus tsked. "My name's been mentioned in passing as they squabble. I keep an eye out for such things."

"How diligent of you."

"Is it true, Prometheus? That this woman of yours was a priestess of ours? That you plotted behind my back to give the humans my power for a mere priestess turned mortal?" Zeus asked so menacingly, so quietly, that even the birds stopped singing. Silence so sharp it engulfed all of them.

Prometheus could have mentioned the others' involvement, but he didn't. Where Amara was concerned, he would always bear the brunt of punishment. He'd turn the world to rubble before he saw her harmed and he entrusted no one else with her safety.

"I did not lie to you. The humans are dying ..."

Zeus stood, rising to his full height, and Prometheus rose with him – not one to back down.

"You lied by omission."

To that Prometheus could say nothing. It was true.

"To dare to try and pull the wool over my eyes ... to make me look a fool. You truly have gone mad."

"I am as sane as I've ever been," Prometheus stated calmly.

Zeus looked at him and continued as if he hadn't heard Prometheus. "It must have been all that time alone that caused it. The first woman you see you decide to ruin the world for! Imagine that! By my name, I should have sent you a dozen whores! It is my fault. I should have given you a punishment the first time, not solitude, but I wanted to see if your allegiance had truly changed over time. Clearly it has not. It will not be a mistake I make again," he warned, pointing a finger at Prometheus.

Stepping out from the table, Zeus began pacing. No doubt he was thinking things through in his head ... or actually discussing them with Athena's mother. Meanwhile, Dionysus leaned back in his chair, a sly curve across his face.

"Why?" Prometheus asked. "What good does your interference bring?"

"I asked myself the same question when you wouldn't let that little priestess of yours die. You ruin my plan, I ruin yours." Dionysus shrugged.

"And how do the goddesses feel knowing that you have ruined their plan too?"

Dionysus shrugged again. "They'll get over it. That's what family does. You wouldn't know that though, would you? After you sold your family out for ours."

"You always were a petty child," Prometheus replied with a look of distaste on his face.

Before Dionysus could retort, Zeus turned back to the table. "Has anyone bar this priestess-turned-mortal been exposed to the white fire?"

"No."

Zeus nodded. "Good. Bring her here to me."

"My friend, you cannot …"

"I am not your *friend*, Prometheus. It is a decree from the King of Gods. If you will not fetch her, in fact – no, you shall not fetch her. I will send Hermes. You are no longer to be trusted. I have given you far too long a leash, but your Titan blood betrays you once again.

You are not to go near this woman until I have spoken to her. That you have betrayed me for a woman, all because you needed to get your cock wet and you wanted her to remember you were a Titan …"

"That was NOT my reasoning." Prometheus growled, for he knew shouting would get him nowhere but he couldn't not speak up. The intention of the white fire offering had never been for his own selfish gains.

Zeus stopped and finally looked Prometheus in the eye. In them, Prometheus saw storm clouds, hurt, and betrayal. A deep sadness etched into eyes of cobalt blue.

"Did you or did you not petition me for the white fire on her behalf?"

Overhead, Zeus' eagle circled and large clouds of thunder began to form.

Prometheus sighed, because, yes, his intention had primarily been to save Amara. He hung his head. Tyche and her good fortune that she'd bestowed upon Prometheus had been wiped out by Dionysus' cunning jealousy and wounded pride.

He felt Zeus' arm curl around his shoulder, a friendly gesture as he delivered a killing blow. "Then you betrayed me. And I am sorry for your actions, for you fought bravely by my side once upon an eon. But now you must pay."

"Zeus—"

"You will wait with the Gorgons until your mortal arrives."

With that, Zeus turned on his leather-bound heel and left. Dionysus followed behind him, whistling, after throwing one last I-told-you-so smirk at Prometheus, who collapsed back into his chair, his head in his hands, his eyes racing behind his eyelids, as he searched his mind desperately for a solution.

CHAPTER XXX

After Prometheus had been summoned away, Amara was not surprised to see a tall, lean god waiting for her against a bulletin board, one of his feet cocked and crossed against his other ankle, as she stepped out of the train carriage onto the platform. Well over six-foot five, Hermes was hard to miss. To humans, he must have looked like a basketball player. To Amara, he was the quickest god in history and, from her returning memory, a complete pain in the arse.

His curls had grown long and were looser than usual, though his beard was neatly trimmed close to his jawline. His slim forehead made way for ledged eyebrows of the same brown hair that had tints of orange when the sun hit it right. His nose had a wide bridge, keeping his eyes slightly further apart. The two of them could pass for brother and sister, albeit with one different parent.

Commuters continued to weave in between and behind the pair of them. The bulletin board Hermes was leaning against promoted the same brand of white trainers that were on his feet. In a slanted red were the words "supreme speed", with the latest Olympic 100 metres winner pretending to dash off in them.

She cocked an eyebrow at Hermes and looked deliberately at his feet.

"Trying to fit in with the humans, are we?"

"Speak for yourself, princess."

Amara scowled. "I'm not a ..."

"... I know what you are. Rumour on the Greek grapevine though is that Prometheus has claimed you as his own."

Amara said nothing to that, choosing instead to turn to her left and walk along the platform. Hermes didn't miss a beat, falling into step with her, one stride for her every two.

"What are you doing here?"

Amara snorted. "Don't be facetious. You know exactly what is going on or you wouldn't be here."

When Prometheus had been taken away, he hadn't even been given the chance to kiss her goodbye. Instead he'd uttered a forlorn two words, "I'm sorry," and departed.

He hadn't even looked back.

She knew he'd done it to protect her from those that watched. That hadn't made it hurt any less. The next day, she'd left Edinburgh.

She had contemplated staying. Athena had told her why they wanted her placed in Scotland before she'd been placed in this human body, which is why she had felt the tug. But Amara, on learning the goddesses had had a lot less information than they let on when they set her on this path, now felt like it was her right to determine where she went from here. And no matter that her priestess memories had returned, the human ones still existed. Being here *hurt*. Being here without *him* hurt.

Saying goodbye at the café had hurt too, though it was more a bittersweet kind of pain. Alice had given her a massive bear hug that had squeezed the breath out of Amara's lungs. Graham, too, had hugged her ... but more with the embrace of a loving father letting his little girl go. The gentleness of which had caused painful tears to spring up in her eyes. Shaking it off, she had made the most of her last day in Edinburgh, making sure each customer received five minutes of her time.

The regulars told her of how they would miss her. Even one of the morning mums had bought her a coffee and a slice of cake to have on her lunch break as a goodbye gift. And then there was Rhonda and Bessie.

"You go after him," Rhonda told her, immediately assuming the reason for Amara's departure before she could say anything else. "You don't let one like that get away." She patted Amara's arm knowingly.

Bessie, meanwhile, handed her a knitted scarf that had been around her own neck.

"To remind you of home here," she had said. And Amara had pretended to be absorbed in the quality of the knitwork to hide the tears that had sprung into her eyes at the kind gesture. Finally, she had found a place that felt like home and now it had been tainted, by those who didn't care.

And while she had understood the goddesses' logic, to birth light in the place that held none any longer, they had been mistaken. The birth of anything was not about the geographical location, it was about *who was present for it.* Namely, family. The emphasis had always been on family. It was why the gods were built of Zeus' lineage, not to obey him – most of them didn't if they could avoid getting caught – but because of the familial blood tie. There was ancient magic in the blood tie, something that had transcended to the humans. Amara could feel it humming in her bones. It was why, in her human form, she had been obsessed with her lineage. The secret to her alchemy had not been to force it but to surround her with the people who would unlock it. And the only person who had helped with that had been sent away.

Which was why, as Hermes found her, she was wearing that knitted purple and white scarf of Bessie's, even though it wasn't *that* cold, as she was on her way back to Father Michel and the Parisian parish in which she'd grown up. Where she'd ran amongst the pews, pretending to hide from the 'demons'.

That young girl had had no idea, she thought, of what the real demons were like. The ones that whispered in your head late at night when no one else was awake to banish them. The ones that were trapped in bottles of liquor that, once escaped, couldn't be coaxed back in. The ones that flogged at her back and made her work like a horse just to believe everything was good enough. The demons she had so desperately tried to keep at bay had appeared to be her friends, her crutches when true evil had entered her life, the fear the goddesses had spoken of.

Except now she had been a human, she could see how easy it was to do. What good had she done with the fear? Nothing. She'd tried to bury it, deep within her. Paper over it, like papier-mâché that at the first sign of water had crumbled. It had taken the white fire of knowledge to begin to burn it away.

She could have chosen to follow Prometheus back to Olympus but that, she acknowledged, would have undone all the sacrifice he had made. She knew how she could spread the message now and knew how to complete her task in a way that would honour his sacrifice. Besides, she didn't want to go back and face those who had used her ... the goddesses. She couldn't do it. The pride she had once felt in serving them had been stripped away with the harsh chemicals of human reality ... and biology.

Now that the white fire had stripped back the barriers to her soul's memories, it was as if everything outside of her was exposed too. Humanity had been stripped of its outer shell and Amara could see all the subconscious thoughts swirling around them within. The conflict they held. The wounds they so desperately clung onto in the hopes no one would hurt them anymore. The projections they put upon each other. The life of the humans was far more brutal than any god in Olympus realised. Only Prometheus had warned her. If only she'd listened.

Amara realised Hermes hadn't spoken and was still following her.

"I'm still a human. I have every right to be here. Hera can't summon me back to berate me when I am the very thing I'm interfering with."

It had taken Amara a solid twelve hours after Prometheus had left to figure out *that* loophole.

"It's not Hera that summons you. It's Zeus."

Amara stopped in her tracks at that. A commuter keeping pace behind her stopped short, bumped into her and muttered disgruntled curses as he tried to weave his way back into the pedestrian traffic around Amara and Hermes.

"My point is still valid," she said, though with such a faint tone even she didn't believe herself.

"Except for the fact you *are* still a member of Olympus. It's not an either/or situation, priestess. It's a both/and."

He had her there.

Amara cleared her throat and tried again.

"I was sent here with a task to do."

"You aren't abandoning your duties by following Zeus' summons," Hermes quipped back. "In fact, from where I'm standing, the only one you are abandoning right now is yourself."

"Excuse me?!" Amara rounded on him.

Hermes rocked back on his heels, his hands in his pockets and shrugged nonchalantly. She continued glaring at him, willing him to explain himself, until he supposedly softened.

"Look, you know how human belief works now. Their world is a reflection of them. Why else would Prometheus abandon you if you hadn't already abandoned yourself? It's time to come home, priestess."

Amara went to open her mouth and closed it again. Then repeated the action, making an excellent impersonation of a goldfish. She knew he was baiting her, trying to get her to agree to come with him. He was using her doubt against her ... wasn't he?

Or was Hermes right?

She knew he was. About the humans at least. That *was* how they operated. Had the abandonment wound, that still felt raw and painful even now she understood it, caused Prometheus to leave her? Had he really been trying to protect her like she thought? Like he said? Had he really been dragged away? Or had it all been a ploy to complete the goddesses' plan? Were they all laughing at her now, back in Olympus? Had Prometheus really been in on it the whole time? Was this the final blow to make her believe in love in order to do their bidding? Because that is what the gods did, she acknowledged. Whatever it took to make sure they got the outcome they wanted was never too much trouble ... for them.

Had she gotten it so very wrong? Or was Hermes playing her now?

"You'll only know if you get the chance to confront him," Hermes said, reading Amara's face like a book. When she blushed, but still made no move to come with him, Hermes delivered the line that tied her hands no matter the answer to her conundrum.

"Trust me, priestess. You aren't going to want to be late for the sentencing."

"Whose?" she demanded.

Hers or Prometheus'? Who had Zeus chosen to punish?

"You'll have to come with me."

CHAPTER XXXI

The sentencing was held in the auditorium, a large, draughty oval room found at the top of Mount Olympus. Held up by large white pillars, the dome had walls but no door, so the mountain breeze swirled through it until Amara could see dust spiralling in the sunlight. As she walked forward, her sandals slapped gently against the marble flooring of the purest white laced with onyx streaks. The sound of her feet bounced off the walls, painted in a blood red around her. Rumour had it Zeus had insisted on the colour in case any blood needed to be shed. Given the frostiness breathing through the auditorium, which had nothing to do with the weather, she could see why.

Ahead of her, there were twelve thrones in a semicircle, each carved from marble that matched the floor and the columns around them. Of course the two closest to the middle were the largest, one slightly bigger than the other still, to represent the King and Queen. Actually, now Amara came to look at it, her eyes sharpening as they squinted, she could see that each chair was sculpted and adorned according to each owner.

To the left of Zeus' throne was one that rose up on a wave – Poseidon. Next to his was Demeter's with maize growing up the throne back. Beside her was Apollo's, a bow and arrow carved into either arm and the sun above his seat. Next to his chair was his twin sister's, Artemis', who also had the bow and arrow, as well as the moon, engraved on hers. Beside that was Athena ... an owl sculpture carved into one arm of her chair, as if it perched there forever.

On the other side, to the right of Hera's throne was Ares ... bloodshed and war scenes etched into his. Beside him, Hephaestus had flames licking up his chair. Next to his was his wife's, Aphrodite's, adorned with roses. Next to hers was Hermes, his staff resting against his chair. And finally there was Dionysus', which had the markings of a grapevine growing over it.

Hermes' words echoed in Amara's mind as she continued walking forward towards the semicircle of thrones. *"Rumour on the Greek grapevine though is that Prometheus has claimed you as his own."*

She gulped. Seven of the chairs were occupied.

She named them in her head as she took deep, steadying breaths and continued to stare straight ahead. *Dionysus, Aphrodite, Ares, Hera, Zeus, Artemis, and Athena.*

Hermes walked beside her until she came level with three women who were huddled to the right of her. She could see that they had someone bound on their knees in chains. When one of them tugged on the chains to force their captive's head back, Amara gasped.

So, it was not to be her sentencing.

Relief and bile rose to the back of her throat as gratitude collided with the grotesque image of Prometheus' face. He'd had one eye gouged out and venomous claw marks down the right side of his face that had penetrated bone. She went to take a step towards him but Hermes' hand on her forearm stopped her. It was only then, when he shook his head, his eyes bowed, that she realised Prometheus was being held by the Gorgons. She immediately averted her gaze and heard them cackle.

Hermes took his seat and Amara was left standing on her own.

"The priestess herself," Zeus rumbled. "So this is who one of my oldest friends would betray me for."

This was not a good start.

She was careful not to look any of them in the eye, particularly her patron goddesses, for fear they saw her seething hatred for them in her eyes. Instead, she dropped into a bow so deep she may as well have been sitting on the floor.

"Rise, child," Hera commanded coldly.

Hera was swathed in layers of blue and green silks. Her hair was pulled back under a heavy gold crown that was encrusted with teardrop emeralds and sapphires. The veil was thinly woven gold, so thin that it looked like the Queen was enshrouded in gold dust.

Next to her, Zeus wore a plain white toga that wrapped over one shoulder and around his groin, leaving his scarred torso otherwise bare. Each scar was a proud battle wound that depicted how Zeus had won his seat and the white of his toga was so bright it dazzled.

They were a formidable pair.

"Well it appears everyone is here, unless the Moirai deign to join us?" Hera asked haughtily, her voice high and cold as it echoed throughout the chamber.

"No, my Queen." For she was not his love. Zeus truly loved no one but himself. Hera, his queen, wife, and sister did not love him either, not like she once had. But she loved the power he wielded and afforded her and so it was a marriage of benefit for both. For a king must have a queen for his legacy and a queen must have her power.

"A pity," Hera muttered, though she could say no more than that. The Moirai answered to no one, least of all the gods. Theirs was a role unto themselves, even if their actions had been the initial cause of this hearing.

"Athena, present your case."

"My Lady." Athena stepped forward off her throne and turned, taking a bow courteous enough to show her respect to Hera but not so deep as to say they were not family. It was a subtle political manipulation, as Athena was not Hera's daughter, but the public acknowledgement that she considered her so should swing her some favour. If there was one thing everyone knew Athena was good at, it was reading political situations with care.

Hera smiled.

"Pray tell, what was the Goddess of Wisdom's logic in sending a priestess to Earth to roam amongst the humans when it had been expressly forbidden by me?"

"I hoped to save my father from heartache."

"Oh?"

"Humans are a dying breed. Their lack of faith in anything other than themselves has brought them to the edge of collapse. I didn't wish to see something that we all so carefully curated being destroyed."

"A dutiful daughter."

The coldness in Hera's tone was not to be missed. Humans had brought more pain – or more accurately wounded pride – to Hera than anything else.

"Granted, they are nothing more than pawns, my Lady. But surely it is better that our amusements are put on them rather than squabble amongst ourselves again?" Athena asked.

After the weaver, the one who had challenged Athena, had so cunningly displayed how the gods used and discarded others, there had almost been a mutiny. Tithes and sacrifices had dropped and Olympus had been on the brink of war, for bartering was how they got things done around here. The humans had also been a convenient way of allowing the gods to have their fun without ruining their society ... and Hera did like the life of luxury that power afforded her. No one had suspected her imposed hiatus on them to last forever.

"And what of you two?" Hera asked, looking between Aphrodite and Artemis, her delicate hands curled over her throne and her thin forearms, where you could practically see bone, coiled and ready to strike.

Aphrodite spoke first.

"The beloved priestess has suffered more than we would have wished. We would not have done so if we did not think it was truly necessary."

"And it was necessary to not ask for my permission, was it?"

"We wished to disrupt life here as little as possible and vanquish unseen foes with as little detection as possible, my Lady," Artemis intervened.

Hera paused for a moment, taking one of her hands and playing it along the gold bangles that decorated her wrists. A nervous gesture for someone not truly comfortable with power that was not her own or a calculated way to make them suffer in silence, it was not clear.

"And you, what say you Prometheus?"

One of the Gorgons pulled the Titan by the thick chain around his neck to his feet and kicked him in the back to push him forward. Prometheus bowed his head as he dropped to one knee. Hera smiled, clearly pleased with the depth as a mark of his respect. Then he raised his head and made eye contact with his one good eye. Defiant as ever.

"My Lady, King, it needs not be said how I feel about the mortals."

Hera's laugh was like a tinkle that froze blood. "No, I suppose not."

"While I was privy to the goddesses' plans, my intention had been to find the priestess and return her to you before any unnecessary damage had been done."

"But you didn't, did you?" Hera purred. "Why Dionysus here claims that he caught you drinking with the priestess but a fortnight ago."

The god in question shot a coy smile at Prometheus once Hera wasn't looking.

"You will have to forgive me, my Lady. I made an error of judgement."

A stunned silence broke out across the auditorium.

"You, the bearer of foresight, made an error of judgement?" Hera asked incredulously.

"How?" she demanded when Prometheus held his silence.

"I didn't anticipate falling in love with her."

All eyes quickly swivelled to Aphrodite.

"What is the meaning of this?" Hera demanded.

Aphrodite rose from her throne. "My Lady, when our priestess was exposed to the fear of humans, I did what I must to protect her. Our intention was for her to eradicate the fear. Unfortunately, events occurred and I was forced to intervene. Ares will attest to that."

Aphrodite waved a hand towards her lover, who nodded once in agreement.

"I did indeed bear witness to the intervention. Aphrodite was well within her rights as the patron of love," he stated before yawning and flexing his muscles.

"And as I can tell you all, only love can drive out fear once it's taken root in the humans. Given that Prometheus was hell-bent on finding the priestess, it was my only solution."

"Why not simply send love throughout the humans if it could eradicate this fear?" Zeus finally asked, apparently no longer bored of this meeting.

"The love has to be pure, Father. So rare is it these days that humans trust the purity of love from another now that they have commercialised and packaged it."

"And how did you know she would trust Prometheus' love?"

"I didn't. But the Moirai assured me that I was making the right moves."

"A gamble nonetheless," Zeus acknowledged, stroking his beard.

"All games in love are a gamble, Father."

"A gamble that has cost us greatly, Daughter. For it seems your love-struck Prometheus here took matters into his own hands."

Zeus' piercing blue eyes landed on his old friend and confidant and all eyes swung back to Prometheus.

Zeus stroked his beard before sighing. "I did not know it was for love."

Prometheus' knees began to buckle.

"And she really is quite a beauty," he mused, clearing his throat when Hera cast him a glacial stare.

"But did you or did you not deceive your King in order to present your priestess with the white fire of knowledge from the tree of life?"

A hushed silence fell over the auditorium.

"I did," Prometheus acknowledged quietly.

"And did you, or did you not, do so knowing the consequences?"

Murmurs broke out amongst those at the hearing.

"SILENCE," Zeus roared.

"I did."

"It pains me to do this, old friend, but you have left me no choice. You knew after the last time you were insubordinate that, should you be punished again, it would echo throughout the heavens. I need your punishment to serve as a reminder to everyone of exactly what I am capable of. Even for old friends."

"I understand," Prometheus said softly, a small smile on his face. He had known his fate before he'd walked in here. Had known it all along if he'd been honest with himself. He just hadn't wanted to see it.

"I, Zeus, decree that you will spend the rest of your days tied to the crag on the mountaintop you stole from, that your liver be ripped from your chest cavity as an act of purification and your eyes pecked out by the birds for your lack of foresight. You will serve your sentence for—"

"Wait."

CHAPTER XXXII

Amara could feel Prometheus' eyes burning into her skin from behind her, warning her to keep quiet. No one was ever foolish enough to interrupt Zeus.

"I a-ap," Amara cleared her throat, took a deep breath and tried again. There was no room for stuttering when negotiating with the gods.

"I apologise for interrupting you, oh King of Gods, but I could not have it on my conscience that Prometheus be punished for a crime that has not borne fruit."

A brief pause of silence that said they were listening, likely to see what was so important that it could break a decree, gave Amara the confidence to continue.

"While it is true Prometheus did present me with the white fire of knowledge, and while I retain human skin, I too retain my memories once again as a priestess thanks to the fire. I was already aware of its existence, so I do not technically fall under the same laws as the humans. And no other human became aware of the knowledge of the fire. I put the embers out of the piece Prometheus brought me rather than sharing that knowledge. No other human knows of its existence ..." As the words died on her lips, Amara realised the magnitude of what she was saying and who she was saying it to.

This time the silence was interrupted by Hera's harsh laugh. "Foolish girl, my husband already knows no other has seen the white fire."

"He does?" Amara said softly as she cocked her head quizzically to the side and looked at Zeus, who chuckled in turn.

Why then had they let her talk?

"You are an inquisitive one. Brave too. I see why my daughters picked you, why Prometheus fell for you."

"You are too kind." Amara dropped her head, her eyes racing as she tried to piece it all together.

Zeus regarded her with a look underneath bushy eyebrows. "And yet I sense a but."

Amara's eyelashes flicked up in surprise. Because there was a but, she just hadn't intended on saying it.

"You may as well speak while you have the floor priestess," Zeus cajoled.

Amara got the distinct impression she was being played with. Like a lazy lion who pretends he isn't about to tear you to shreds, Zeus seemed languid.

"You would be punishing the wrong god."

Hermes let out a low whistle, Ares a bark of a laugh.

"You dare ..." Athena breathed.

Amara took a deep breath and finally looked at her, at each of the goddesses in turn.

"What you all did was neither wise, nor loving, nor protective. You asked for honour and obedience in traits you did not show. It was not Prometheus' doing but yours that sent me to Earth. But all the things you claimed to cloak me with were only provided to me by Prometheus in my short time there."

"Amara," Prometheus warned.

"Silence," one of the Gorgons hissed, a brutal tug on the chain around his neck bringing him back to his knees.

Amara continued, her mind made up and her voice strong, the residue of the black tar of fear inside her bones bubbling until it began to burn away completely. "You, Lady Aphrodite, claim that you were doing the Moirai's bidding. But then so did you, Lady Athena, when you gave me this task. Yet you both had your own motivations. This was about more than saving the humans. You sought your father's approval, Lady Athena, as always. That much is clear to me from what you've just said now. And you, Lady Aphrodite, sought to get your way once again. And you both used me in the process because that's what the gods and goddesses, like you, do. Use others for their own selfish gain and claim it is because of the Fates. For all I know they never even spoke to you.

For my entire existence I have served you both – and you, Artemis – loyally. But this is not a moira, a destiny, I would have ever chosen for myself. I no longer fear being cast aside by you. Should I now choose, I would choose the

283

only one who actually aided me in a time of need. He who is taking the punishment for your failings.

And you, oh King of Kings and God of Gods, are letting them."

The auditorium once again fell silent. All Amara could hear was her heart hammering against her ribcage, the blood roaring in her ears and simultaneously draining all colour from her face. Her body shook, her fingers tingled, her legs felt as if they were about to give out. Always she had been the pleaser, in both priestess and human form. Always, she had tried to be what was right and good in this world, her greatest fear being cast aside or abandoned by those she loved and respected. But now she knew what that was like and she'd survived it. So to Hades she would go, with those who had put her through it. No more.

"An insolent one, isn't she?" Hera mocked in a high-pitched, sing-song tone that was as eerie and creepy as it was cutting.

"I dare say Prometheus has rubbed off on her," Athena added, her grey eyes clouded over. A storm, about to break.

"She should be flogged for the way she speaks to my sisters and I," Artemis added.

Aphrodite didn't say anything, the complex confusion on her face utterly mesmerising as if she battled internally with herself about what to say.

Finally, Zeus spoke.

"Be that as it may, priestess, Prometheus still disobeyed me."

"But—"

"Silence. You have said your piece. Interrupt me again and I will have you serve your time with Hades."

Amara snapped her lips shut.

"But, for your bravery in defending a man we both once called friend, I will ask my wife to spare your life," Zeus continued before turning to Hera. "Her fate is otherwise yours, my Queen."

Amara's gaze flew to Hera's, whose smile turned cruel in an upward sneer. She paused for a few minutes, letting the weight of silence engulf them all, dread filling Amara's bones.

"My husband may have spared your life but you still broke my rule."

"No," Amara whispered to herself, her eyes widened in horror as she realised what Hera meant. When she had first met Prometheus and he had asked what would become of her should she be caught, Athena had said she would not be done for meddling, for the rule only applied to gods. Except she'd just condemned Athena and her sisters, and now they sat stoically watching on as Hera unleashed her anger on the only person in the room she was allowed to whip.

"You will be exiled from Olympus and consumed by your mortal flesh," the Queen continued.

"NO!" Prometheus shouted.

"Hold your tongue," Hera hissed, her face contorting into a vile, pinched expression that belied her true nature. When he went to bite back a rebuttal, she interrupted him.

"Gorgons, if you can't restrain him, take him away," Hera said coldly. "As for the humans, they too shall pass into extinction. We will have new toys created in their place." A pointed glance at Zeus in affection. "Artemis and Aphrodite, you both, with Athena, shall pay the patronages for these new toys, given your meddling. The others here present bear witness to this."

With that, Hera clapped her hands and the sentencing passed.

Pulling against the chains, Prometheus rose to his feet, tugging against the full force of the three Gorgons, and carried himself towards Amara and cupped her face in his roughly calloused hands.

"She may bind you to mortal flesh but she cannot eradicate your soul. Your essence is immortal. Do you hear me, Amara?"

Her eyes pooled with tears as she nodded and placed her hands gently either side of his cheeks, desperately trying to take him in, to remember every inch of him.

"You will find another mortal body and *I will find you.* In every lifetime, my love. It may not be in this one, or even in the next century, but I will find you. You must stay strong. You must fight, even when the days seem bleak and the nightmares come." He wiped away tears that dashed down her cheeks. Understanding dawned as his foresight rose once more to the fore.

"Have hope, my love. I will survive this. You will be the reason that I do, but promise me you will fight."

Amara nodded, unable to say anything, Prometheus' face blurry behind her tears. She desperately wanted to see him, to memorise every crease and crack in his skin. Instead, her hands followed the contours of his face, as if reading him in Braille before touching a desperate salted kiss to his lips.

Two of the Gorgons stepped forward, taking either arm of Prometheus as he was led from the auditorium. Denied even the chance to watch him walk away, Amara clenched her fists, her shoulders hitched. She flinched as she heard the crack of a whip through the air meet flesh and Prometheus let out a painful groan as the Gorgons cackled. Their laughter died in the wind.

"Come," Hermes said to Amara, having appeared at her side. "I will take you back to Earth."

CHAPTER XXXIII

It had been a year since Amara had been banished back to Earth, to serve the remainder of her existence, when she found herself in the exhibition section of the library where she had met Prometheus. It seemed like a lifetime ago. Her immortality bound to human life had taken on a new quality now she knew that there really was a death at the end of her sentence, even if it came with rebirth in a new body. An everlasting hell on Earth.

Prometheus' words reverberated in her ears. *There would be other lifetimes.* At the time, her faith in him, in his words, had been unwavering. But Chronos had a funny way of making time fade all things. Even a year in human terms seemed both too short to change anything and yet held the potential to change everything.

Now, when grief consumed her and Dionysus tried to tempt her with wine, she would go to reach for the bottle and stop herself. It took conscious effort to pull back, close her eyes, and think of her love, of their time together, of being reunited once more. After a year of this, she had finally woken with a decision.

Smoothing her hands over her emerald-green dress that fell to her knees in playful pleats, Amara continued to walk around the exhibition, perusing the ancient lost treasures it housed, restored to their former glory. She stopped at a podium in the middle of the room. Inside the protective glass container was the most beautiful box. It must have originally been ornamented with jewels, but those had fallen away over the years and cracks and dents had aged the box. And yet, someone had taken the care to lace every indent with gold until it looked as if the box had always meant to be that way.

Amara bent down to read the label. 'A take on Pandora's box' it read. Of course, Pandora's box had been real. Amara had seen it when she was back in Olympus. It had been given to the first woman. She, in turn, had been presented to Prometheus' brother as a bride and – in her desperate curiosity – had released the first evils on the Earth. The only thing, according to legend, that hadn't escaped was hope.

Amara snorted. *The history books had got something right at least.*

"It's beautiful, isn't it?" A petite Asian woman, whose lanyard around her neck indicated she worked here, gestured to the case inside the glass pillar.

"Yes," Amara replied truthfully.

"Don't you just love the idea that hope cracked it open, and humans pieced it back together?"

At Amara's puzzled look, the woman pointed to the handwritten note underneath the exhibit that said the same thing. Amara's breath hitched. She'd recognise that writing anywhere. It was his.

Had he really written it all that time ago? Had he known? Had he foreseen what she was about to do? Is that what he meant when he had asked her to fight?

The exhibit guide continued talking but Amara wasn't listening. Instead she made her excuses, walked out the door and through the winding paved stone streets that led her to the little cottage she had decided to rent near the city.

They had all been wrong that day in the auditorium, herself included. Prometheus' love hadn't eradicated the fear in her. Standing up to the goddesses hadn't done it either. For when she had been banished back on Earth, she could feel the inky blackness of fear claw at her human skin once again. Alchemy alone didn't stop it. The hope Prometheus had literally gifted her did.

But the only way to have hope was to crack everything else it came with open ... and let the humans piece the world back together in a way even more beautiful than before.

She had lied through her teeth that day in the auditorium. When they'd so brutally punished her and Prometheus for their own crimes. And they'd thought her too insignificant, too slight in power, to lie to them.

Entering the cottage, Amara walked down the corridor to the second door on her left, where her bedroom was. Next to the bed was a tall, thin white cupboard door that barely classified as a wardrobe. Inside it, at the bottom, on the grey carpeted floor, was a shoebox. Inside the shoebox was a candle that glowed with a white flame that flickered purple and blue, and never burnt out.

The white fire of knowledge was only a gift if you knew what to do with it. At first she had contemplated spreading the white fire through the Earth. It would consume everything, a never-ending blaze, and chaos would reign. Penance for being ripped away from her love. But then Hera would get her wish, humanity destroyed in a fire that would burn Earth to its core, and Amara wasn't about to let that bitch get anything more than she'd already taken.

No, instead, Amara had decided to do everything she could to protect and nurture those that her love had given his life for. Twice. And hoped that one day, when he was released, he would once again be reunited with his creations in their original form ... back to their true natures.

The white fire, shared with those who were ready to remember, would be the valve for humanity. It would burn away what didn't serve, release some of the pressure, prune that which was dead. It would reintroduce the humans to a world where they would not be slaves to themselves or the gods' whims.

She simply had to find those lost souls who knew they needed something. With the goddesses' eyes no longer upon her, no longer believing her necessary, she would work unnoticed amongst the humans to find them and share what she knew. She would share with them the herbs it would take to cure ailments their medicines couldn't. How to invoke the favour of the gods they chose to follow with simple offerings that would get an inclination of respect without being overly obvious. How to purify the lands they had polluted and how to feel at peace within their bones. How to rewrite the scriptures that no longer served them and how to build new systems that would break old ways of being and breathe revitalising energy into their world once again.

It was simple alchemy, elemental work. But then the humans were the only creation made of all the elements. Those who took the teachings and applied them would be able to handle the heat of the white fire and the knowledge it offered, Amara reasoned.

Hers was not a story that would receive glory and accolades. She would not be remembered. But the humans would survive – there was hope yet.

ACKNOWLEDGEMENTS

I t has been the longest time since I have written a book (I published others under a different name), but the process of writing *Prometheus' Priestess* was unlike any other I had experienced before. What started as an idea from a meditation in August 2020 ended up becoming a series of intertwined life experiences and ancient knowledge pulled out through the writing process, Prometheus by my side the entire time. I had learnt some of Amara's lessons before I began writing, so I knew her back story intimately, but many lessons I learnt along the way with her too. And there were some people that were important parts of that journey I would like to thank.

Firstly, to Mary-Kate who received the dedication. Your magic is what allowed Prometheus to speak to me in my head for the first time. I hope you realise how divine you are.

Secondly, to Shaun, whose encouragement and emotional intelligence, strength, and vulnerability, helped me cultivate a connection between these characters that I don't think would have otherwise existed.

To my QM sisters, who held me through the portal of mortal to priesthood. You witnessed the tears, held the space, and offered the support I needed to bring this book to life and tell the story. For that I will be forever grateful.

To my beta readers, Natasha and Chelsea, I owe you more than thanks. You strengthened the story in a way I couldn't see. I adore both of you.

To Jo, who has read every book I have ever written, and whose never-ending faith and encouragement in me floors me every time, I thank you from the bottom of my heart for sticking by me.

To my editor, Jess, and to my proofreader, Bernadette, thank you for being talented at the parts of book editing I hate! You polished this book to a level I could not have done and made it shine. I am so, *so* grateful for you.

To my mum for, well, everything. And particularly for always putting a book in my hand.

Finally, and most importantly, to Bren who gave me the attic to write in – I did it. I finished it.

THE FEMME FATALE SERIES BOOK #2: A LIFETIME KIND OF LOVE

Coming soon...

They say unrequited love is the worst kind of love, but
what of past loves come to this lifetime? What of a
connection that is deeper than one lifetime can allow?

What do you do when they appear?
When you tear each other's wounds anew,
Not recognising how to reconcile in this lifetime?

What then?

How do you move on from a lifetime love
that was eons in the making
And forever in your future?

Explore the first 90 days
meeting a past love affair
Through the ancestry
of Hades & Persephone
in the pages of this poetry

In the hopes that it will
ease your longing
and offer discernment.

GWYNETH LESLEY began her writing journey when she was eight with a poem about 'Seasons' and a short story called 'Chocoholic' that featured a giant on the motorway.

She went on to write several novels and a bestselling novella under another name while she worked in London in all manner of publishing, writing, and editing jobs to hone her craft.

She has also been a massage therapist, waitress, and trauma support specialist ... jobs she credits with making her a better author.

Gwyneth currently resides in New Zealand while working on the Femme Fatale series, a collection of traumatic love stories that haven't been told yet.